Return to Tiffany's

Return to Tiffany's

A Never Too Late Love Story

And three other true short stories of
JEROME MARK ANTIL

ISBN-13: 9780997180244 (TPB)
ISBN-13: 978-0-9971802-5-1 (E-Book)
ISBN: 0997180242

Library of Congress Control Number: 2016918667

Cover Design: Dennis Graham
Copy Editor: Jolene Paternoster
PRINTED IN AMERICA

Stories

Return to Tiffany's

Richard Leaves the Choir Breathless

Postwar Shortages and Shortfalls

A Cazenovia Christmas Past

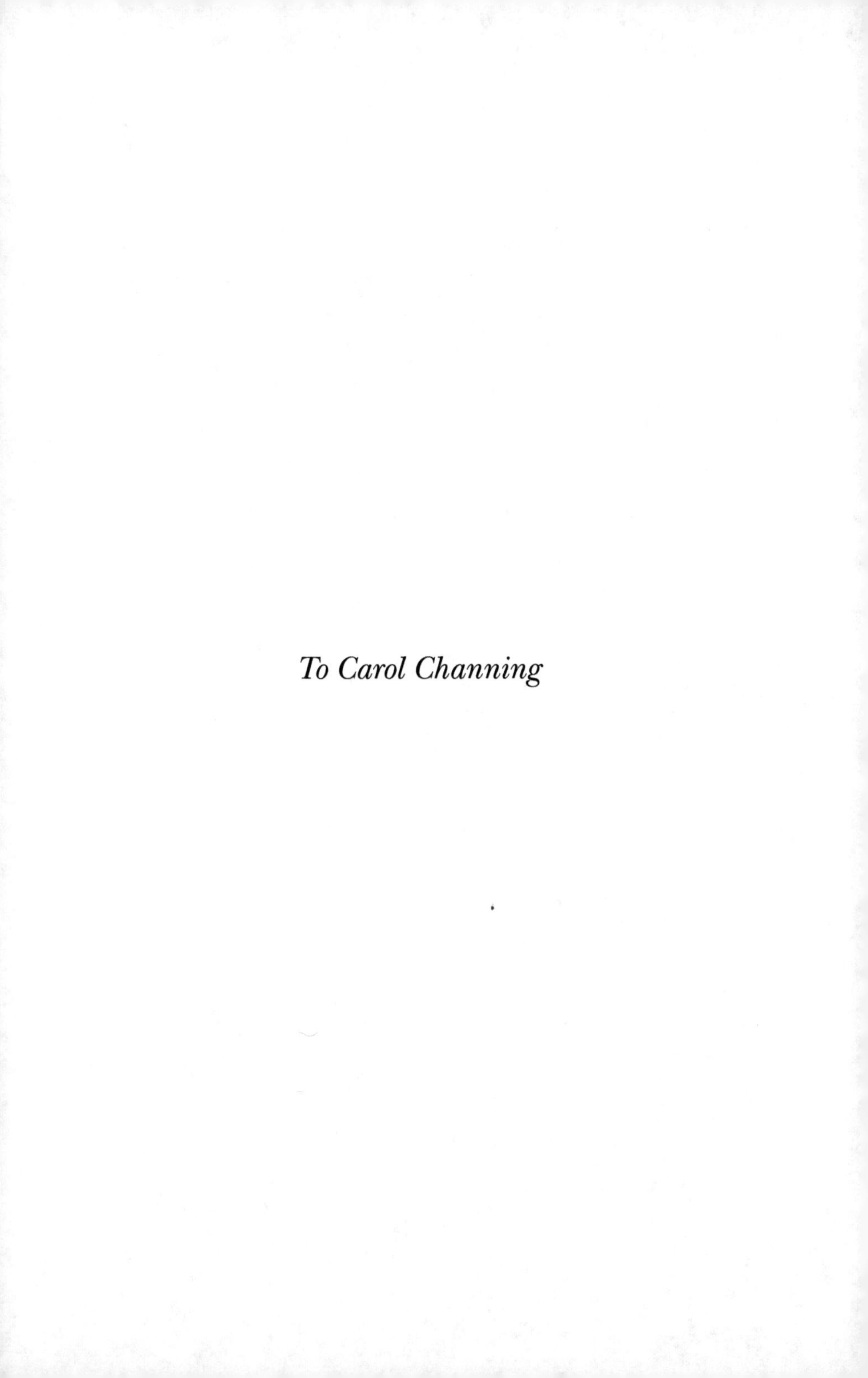

To Carol Channing

RETURN TO TIFFANY'S

I was twenty-five; she was twenty-three. I had traveled to Bellerose, a village on Long Island, from Cincinnati to attend the wedding of a friend, Gregory's sister-in-law. A girl had flown in from Paris to be a bridesmaid for her high school friend. I don't remember whether it was Charlie or Fran—the parents of the bride—who sent me upstairs to their master bedroom to retrieve either a bolt of fabric or some wrapping paper. I can't for the life of me recall who sent me or what the errand was. There was a balcony at the top of the stairs of this lovely, modest Tudor, which gave it a warm, regal elegance. Aromas of authentic Italian sauces and spices wafted from the kitchen below while gentle laughter and what must have been rustling garment-tissue papers signaled that the bridal weekend had begun and charted my course down the second-floor hallway. I remember pausing first on the tall balcony, looking over it, and recalling the Christmastime photographs of it that I'd seen in family-picture albums. I imagined the annual tree towering in the small living room and rising up to meet me at the balcony and making another season bright and alive for every age. The tree wasn't there on that day, of course, but I could see an oversized black-and-white photo of it reflected in the mirror over the mantle, and that made me feel as though it were. It wasn't a long hallway, mind you, and as I approached the first bedroom on the left, I could hear giggling from behind its door, which was slightly ajar and blocking my view of most of the room.

Slowing to a snoopy pace, I saw her for the first time through that crack in the partially open door. She appeared as a dark silhouette—as a slight, apparently naked cameo of a woman with a perfect form standing statuesquely in front of an open Venetian-blinded window. With her arms outstretched, she was anticipating a slip, a petticoat, or, perhaps, a bridesmaid's gown that would soon be handed to her for a fitting. Though I was fixated on her, I reluctantly kept moving down the hall to the master bedroom on the right, where the three packages I'd been asked to bring down to the kitchen lay on the bed. Balancing them in my arms, I returned even more slowly—deliberately slowly that time—back down the hall, listening to the laughter. I looked in, hoping for a chance to see the naked silhouette again, never suspecting that my second look would forever change my life. It was the same girl, all right, but she was no longer in silhouette, as the blinds were no longer open. She wasn't naked at all. Like a goddess, she stood there tall and motionlessly in flesh-colored panties and a bra with lace and cuts and shapes—the kind of bra that one would've found in *Vogue* magazine. This time I could see her golden-blond hair and her striking blue eyes and her face, which was more beautiful than Botticelli's Venus. She was pouting as though she were a schoolgirl experiencing her first Bordeaux in Paris. Never once looking my way, the girl reached for a satin bow on the sill, perhaps for her hair or to keep her hands busy.

Pamela Berkin, model – (from a Shampoo advertisement)

I walked to the balcony, memorizing the face I would never forget, and descended the steps just as the front door opened. As I neared the bottom of the stairs, my friend Gregory walked in and then nudged the door closed with his elbow as he set his suitcase in the entryway. He waved hello with a lifted palm.

I stepped over to him and leaned in discreetly.

"Greg, upstairs, the bridal girls—they're trying on wedding stuff. Hey, man, I just saw absolutely the most beautiful—"

"So you must have met Pamela. Isn't she something?"

Greg looked over the top of his glasses and raised his brow.

"Jesus," I said.

Pamela worked as a model in Paris and had flown in for the wedding. She had a look that guys like me only dreamed about. Then back in her hometown and with the friends she'd grown up with, she was quite natural and seemed like a down-to-earth schoolgirl.

Now, so many years later, I don't remember whether I went to Bellerose just to visit with Gregory and his family and to attend the wedding or to be in the wedding. But I wound up being a groomsman and renting a last-minute black-tie-and-tails outfit that didn't fit my six-foot-ten-inch frame. As I was the tallest male, I was paired with Pamela, who was nearly five foot ten in heels and the tallest female, for the nuptial stroll down the aisle.

I hardly remember the wedding ceremony in the church in Bellerose. It's been fifty years. I do remember noticing that the sleeves of my tuxedo weren't long enough for my arms when I was posing for the wedding photos. I barely remember the reception, which was under a large tent somewhere on Long Island, although I do remember two experiences I had during it. I can't forget my first taste of Swedish meatballs, and I vividly remember meeting Robert F. Kennedy. He was running to be a senator of New York State. Kennedy and his entourage had crashed the reception tent, and he'd walked through it shaking hands and permitting photo ops.

Years later I discovered a photo of Kennedy checking Pamela out while I was standing behind her. I got a copy of the photo and have had it—a picture of the lovely Pamela and me, with Robert F. Kennedy—on a wall in my home ever since.

A snapshot of RFK, Pamela, and me behind her

This wedding day happened in 1966. Pamela flew back to Paris, and I moved on.

For the ten years that followed it, I was busy building my career in marketing, drinking too much, and getting married and divorced. I first worked in King of Prussia, Pennsylvania, at the AAMCO Transmissions headquarters, heading up marketing and using Zsa Zsa Gabor in television commercials. I moved to Dallas, Texas, in 1969 and worked as the vice president of marketing for Bonanza International, the steak-house chain. There I used stars like Lorne Green, Michael Landon, and Dan Blocker for promotional advertising. I traveled more than a hundred thousand miles a year in this country alone. From time to time, I would hear tidbits and rumors from Greg and others about Pamela and what she was up to.

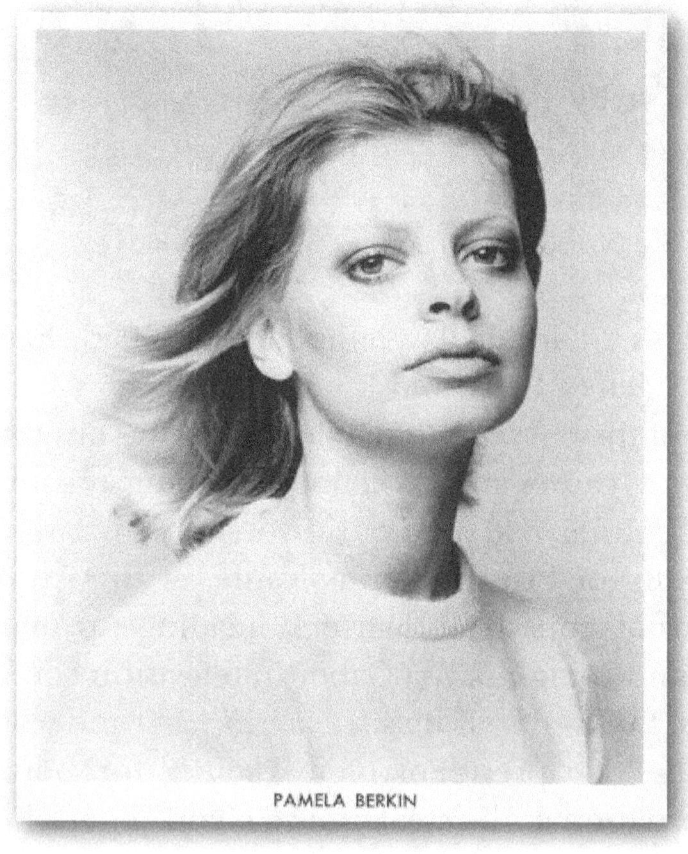

Having returned to New York City, she was under contract with the prestigious, world-class Ford Modeling Agency and was working under Eileen Ford's wing literally around the clock and around the world, modeling for print ads and appearing in dozens of television commercials and as an extra in movies.

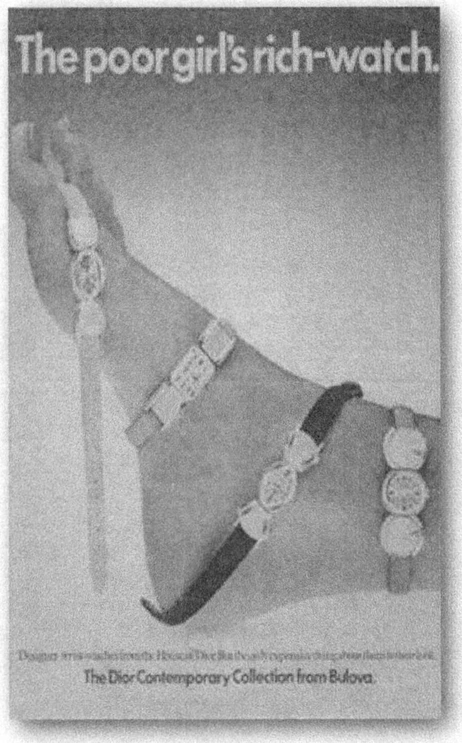

One of Pamela Berkin's feet

Pamela's face, hands, feet, and hair were used in high-fashion shots, and she was among the most photographed women in New York City. She appeared on *The Tonight Show Starring Johnny Carson* four times as a background model and on *The Ed Sullivan Show;* once had tea with George Harrison on a movie set in London—and met all of the other Beatles there; danced with Al Pacino; and turned down Cary Grant the two times he asked her out. She fainted the first time but turned him down nonetheless, as she had a boyfriend, a legendary photographer whom she loved.

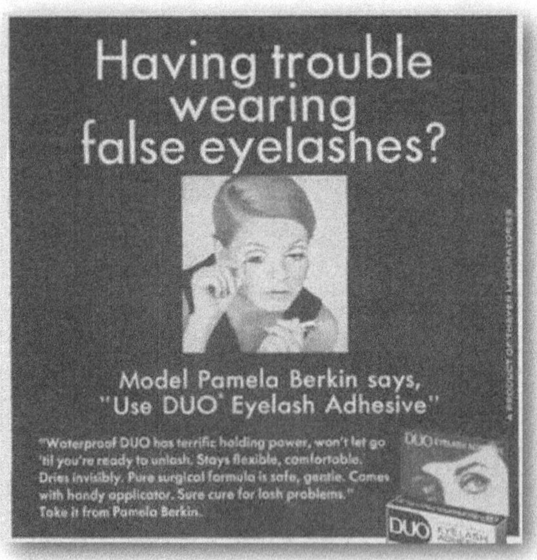

Pamela once shared giggles with Barbara Sinatra in the ladies' room of a famous New York supper club as they held the door closed and smoked cigarettes. Apparently, Frank didn't permit smoking at the table while a singer was performing. She danced with Walter Winchell at the El Morocco, and while she was sitting with her mother and her uncle at a famous New York City piano bar after hours, a young Liberace dressed in beige slacks and a cashmere sweater but no jewelry happened in, sat at the piano, and played for the three of them until dawn. In Paris Pamela dated actor Charles Boyer's son and flew to Rome with him to watch an all-night black-tie symphonic recording session that his father was reading for.

Pamela felt that she was in heaven following a sidewalk lunch in Paris with fashion-world icons Oleg Cassini and Claude Cartier. She recalled feeling like Gigi as the three of them walked arm in arm down the Champs-Élysées, Pamela in a Breton hat, a sleeveless blouse, a buttoned vest, a pleated skirt, and patent-leather shoes. In New York, Sylvia and Ed Sullivan were among her best friends, and she, Sylvia, and Ed would frequently dine together, travel, and test their talents at track betting windows. Between shoots she studied tap at Carnegie, took drafting classes at NYU, and worked part time for an architect.

Pamela had many male friends who were not lovers. At a supper party in a Manhattan brownstone, her friend and escort Franco Occhiuzzi, the New York correspondent for *Corriere della Sera* in Milan, introduced Pamela to the host, the Italian film director Federico Fellini. Fellini stood awkwardly from his seat at the table, took Pamela's hand, and kissed it. "You are so like my wife," he said. "There's sadness in your eyes." Dustin Hoffman once sat on a picnic blanket with Pamela and some other extras during a shooting break in *Marathon Man*. It seemed that each time I was in New York, I would see her image all about on posters and bus cards and in the pages of the *New York Times* or Sunday magazine sections.

Pamela in a Parisian magazine

It appeared to me that Pamela was to Paris and New York City what the English model Twiggy was to London at the time.

Pamela was still the most beautiful woman I had ever met. For more than a decade, I had neither the opportunity nor the nerve to look her up or to even invite her to lunch.

In 1976 I was negotiating with Colonial Penn, which wanted to buy a list of more than a million senior-citizen mail-order buyers that my publishing company owned. The company wanted the names of proven senior mail-order buyers so that it could promote its insurance division and recruit members for AARP, which was in its infancy at the time. Colonial Penn was in Philadelphia, but I had flown to New York City, having decided that I would have some fun while in town. My plan was to go see Greg, to maybe have dinner, to make the Big Apple my overnight base, and to commute down to Philadelphia by train the next morning to see Colonial Penn. I wouldn't be in the city long enough to go to Connecticut to see his family. My secretary had booked reservations for me at The Algonquin. The Checker cab I was in made its way from LaGuardia to my first stop, his offices at the General Motors building at Fifty-Eighth and Fifth.

By that time Greg was a huge deal and a VP with Revlon, the health-and-beauty aid and cosmetic giant. He worked in the large corner office on the forty-ninth floor, overlooking Madison Avenue and Fifty-Eighth.

I was in the city for a night in 1976.

"Jerry! What're you doing in town?" Greg asked. "Ivy, hold all my calls."

He pushed the door closed behind us and hugged me like I was a brother from another mother.

"How come you didn't call?" he asked.

"It was last minute."

"Bad night, Jer. I have a dinner meeting with Larry at Giraffe. We're going over numbers. I can't get out of it."

"No problem," I said.

"Why don't you go grab something at P. J.'s, and when I'm done, we'll meet. Later we can ride up to Greenwich. You can see the kids. Stay a few days."

"Can't. I have to be in Philadelphia the first thing in the morning. I'm at the Algonquin and have to catch an early train. I thought we'd maybe have a drink or dinner."

"So go to P. J's, and I'll catch you tomorrow. When're you coming back from Philly?"

"I'm not. I go from Philly to Cleveland for a creditors' meeting. Good seeing you, Greg. I'll head over to the hotel and check in—maybe eat there. I don't much feel like doing the P. J. Clarke's scene alone."

"Why don't you call Pamela?"

"Huh?"

"Pamela. You remember Pamela. She lives a block from here. Take her to P. J's."

"You've got to be shitting me. Pamela Berkin would never consider going out with me."

"Well, not if you put it that way, she wouldn't. Call and ask her to grab a burger at P. J.'s. She'll remember you from Bellerose."

"I don't know."

"Jer, did I ever tell you what Lauren Hutton told me?"

"The famous Revlon model? That Lauren Hutton?"

"That's her."

"No. What?"

"She told me that most of the guys she would've liked to go out with never asked her, thinking they wouldn't stand a chance."

"Really?"

"Call Pamela. Here's her number. I see her carrying her portfolio around the agencies on Madison Avenue all the time, and she's usually alone when she runs from shoot to shoot."

I picked up Greg's office phone and called Pamela nearly ten years to the day after I'd met her for the first time. She told me that of course she remembered me—I was the tall fellow—and that yes, she'd love to see me. She gave me her address, said that she lived in 5W, and told me to come on over.

Pamela, exhausted after a shoot

Her building on Fifty-Eighth Street looked like an old city mansion. Inside the back hallway was an iron elevator like the one Audrey Hepburn and Cary Grant use in *Charade*. The fifth-floor hallway appeared to be fifteen feet tall or taller. The door to 5W opened, and there was Pamela, standing like the carefree Holly Golightly from *Breakfast at Tiffany's*, wearing a curled, fleece-lined gray sweatshirt that exposed one lovely shoulder; pink shorts; and bare feet with two coats of fine red nail polish on her toes.

I kissed her cheek and followed her into her one-room, one-bath apartment.

"Pardon the mess," Pamela said. "I just got home from a shoot that started at five thirty this morning."

"Hey, if you're tired, maybe this isn't—"

"I'm not tired, Jerry—just winding down. It takes a while."

The apartment was a nice size despite the fact that there was only one room, and the bathroom was nearly as large as the main room, with a porcelain tub sporting commanding claw feet on tiptoe. The ceilings were taller than fifteen feet and edged with bold but intricate, ornate moldings that matched the walls' wainscoting. Despite its size, the apartment was impeccably decorated and showcased a stout Louis XIV–style bureau that Pamela had purchased for $150 from a friend who had moved out of the city. Well-appointed prints hung on the walls, and a refrigerator that looked like it was from the twenties stood guard. I looked at the ceiling and walls as if I were in a museum, occasionally copping a glance of Pamela—of those blue eyes, her hair, her bare shoulder, and her lips, which she pouted at every opportunity. I couldn't believe I was with her…I was Pamela's date.

"Can I offer you a drink?"

"What've you got?"

She led me over to her refrigerator, opened the door, and leaned in as though she were Alice in Wonderland glancing through the looking glass.

"Well, I have peanut butter, and I have mayonnaise, and I have scotch. I have two bottles of Chardonnay, and I have gin. Uh, no. My mistake. It's Stoli."

"Scotch and water," I said as I backed away and sat down on the sofa.

Pamela and I sat and talked about our travels, the wedding, and our other adventures over one drink and then another and perhaps even more.

"What do you feel like eating?" I asked. "Where should we go?"

"I don't know."

"Greg suggested P. J. Clarke's."

"Not really that hungry—at least not yet."

"Is that a backgammon set over there by the wall? Don't tell me you play backgammon."

"Oh, yes. Backgammon keeps me from going crazy when I'm on set. I either read books or play backgammon with someone between shoots. The wait between shoots can be endless, with all of the lighting and the props. Do you play?"

"Ever played strip backgammon?" I said.

"Strip backgammon! Strip backgammon, eh? Why, you filthy, disgusting pig," Pamela said.

"No worries—not if you're good. Depends on how much confidence you have in the roll," I said.

"That's no fair, though. You have cuff links and a tie. You already have the advantage."

I tilted my drink back, an ice cube clanking into my mouth, and set the glass down. I crunched on the cube, unsnapped my cuff links, and set them on the side table. I removed my tie and cavalierly dropped it to the floor like a gauntlet.

"Why, you are a naughty," Pamela said, smirking. "You probably have a T-shirt on under your shirt, and I just have this sweatshirt."

"My shirt and T-shirt will be one item."

"Let me order pizza," Pamela said. "What do you like?"

Pamela stood up and walked over to her Princess phone, which was resting on the bureau. I stood, stepped over the coffee table, and followed her. She turned around.

"I know I like you," I said. "Always have." I cupped her face in my hands, leaned down, and kissed the lips I'd dreamed of kissing for all of those years. They were just as sweet as I'd imagined. She was startled, but she liked the kiss. I could tell she did when she rolled her eyes back like Audrey Hepburn does in *How to Steal a Million*, with Peter O'Toole. Audrey sinks down and into a cab. Pamela dreamily closed and opened her eyes and gently pushed the phone receiver, then in her hand, into my chest.

"Go sit down, and behave." She smiled.

She dialed the phone number from memory and asked for an extra-large plain pizza and a bag of ice cubes, if they could manage it.

The next thing I remember is waking up in her bed—which was the sofa bed turned out—looking up at the beautiful molding framing the high ceiling, and briefly wondering where I was. I jogged my memory and raised my wrist and looked at my watch. I had just thirty-five minutes to get to Penn Station, where I would catch the train to the Thirtieth Street Station in Philadelphia.

I glanced about the quiet morning and room. Just inside the bathroom door, Pamela was standing on a cream–colored wooden step stool completely awake and naked, busily adjusting the new shower curtain hanging over the porcelain tub.

I pulled my socks on, dressed quickly, found my cuff links and tie, and stepped into the bathroom behind Pamela.

"Morning," I said.

"Why, good morning to you," she said, not taking her eyes off of the hook she was fitting to the shower rod.

"Need the shower?"

Gently holding her hips, I kissed her on the small of her back. "Pretty Holly Golightly, I've got to run," I said.

"Oh, I do love *Tiffany's*," Pamela said, opening a hook for the shower curtain. "Remember that fabulous black dress she wore in the pastry and Tiffany window scene? Those shoes? It was Givenchy—Givenchy always dressed Audrey. Givenchy is so divine. I wore him in Paris. Get some pizza—we never touched it last night."

I kissed my fingertips, reached up, and softly touched Pamela's lips, letting her kiss my fingertips good-bye as I stepped from the bathroom and lifted the lid of the pizza box on the coffee table. The only slice missing was the one Pamela had eaten that morning. I grabbed a piece in one hand and my briefcase and carry-on bag in the other and departed.

"Bye, baby doll."

"Bye, Tall Jerry. You're fun. Don't make it ten years next time."

For the thirty-five years following that evening to remember, we were nearly fifteen-hundred miles apart—I was in Dallas, and Pamela, in New York City. I was as consumed by business as Pamela was by her career. I drank too much; bought and sold businesses in trouble; had a bout with bleeding ulcers; was named "bachelor of the month" in *Cosmopolitan* at thirty-seven; got married at thirty-eight; and had a baby girl at forty-two. Four years later, some IRS agents came to the door, asking me for more money than I could have paid them in years. I'd been on the board of directors of a company in Houston the owners of which had never told me that they hadn't paid their withholding taxes. Soon after that visit came the divorce proceedings.

One night my daughter—who was four and a half at the time—had her grandmother get me on the telephone. Aware of the divorce and in tears, she made me promise her three things. First, she made me promise that I would never tell her a fib. Second, she made me promise that I would never miss a visitation (they were every two weeks). Third, she made me promise that I would tell her stories of what the world had been like when I'd grown up. I promised to meet her every request. For three years, I drove ten hours every other Friday, picked her up in Beaumont, and brought her to my home in Austin, where I'd found work. I drove another ten hours every other Sunday to bring her home. For two years I worked in Toronto, Canada, and was at her doorstep in southeast Texas every other Friday at three o'clock to take her to my hotel, and

I never missed one visit. For four years, I worked in Red Bank, New Jersey, and was at her home in Beaumont every other Friday. I never missed one.

During that time I would not let myself be distracted from my promises to my daughter. If I met a lady on a plane or in my travels, I would have a polite conversation with her and then toss her card into a wastebin so that I wouldn't be tempted to break my promises to my little one. She was in high school when I finally paid off the IRS. Well into my sixties, I worked in Dallas on a lifetime agreement, heading up marketing for the nation's largest travel publisher and did some adjunct lecturing at Cornell University on tourism's impact on the economy.

On Thanksgiving Day when I was sixty-eight, my life molted. My friend Greg had called me earlier and invited me to Raleigh to spend Thanksgiving with the family. Holidays can be a lonely time for a single man; for an old single man they just seem quiet even if that man has a workload and commitments to a project at Cornell University concerning a study on tourism. I decided that I wanted some noise, so I made arrangements to fly into Raleigh on Thanksgiving morning and to meet Greg and the family at a party and dinner that they'd be attending. There was the typical holiday catching up and pretending that you remember all of the old times. By that stage in my life, I had begun my writing career and was working with a freelance editor from a Simon & Schuster subsidiary, Baen Books. I was basically writing crap, and she was turning it into fertilizer, but even after her editing, it was still crap. A Thanksgiving football game was playing on the oversized television screen, which turned the otherwise lovely living room into a rec room; there was music filtering in from another room, and many of us stood around listening to both and celebrating good cheer and the organized dysfunction of the party. It was well into this gathering and among the clanking of ice cubes and the block of cheddar being cut that the bride from Bellerose all those many years ago walked over to me in the parlor.

"Jerry, do you remember Pamela?"

"Pamela. Oh yes. How could I forget? Do I remember Pamela."

"She's a widow now."

"Oh my."

She rambled on about Pamela's husband and about music and continued to murmur about things that I didn't hear, as I was thinking back to my night with Pamela and to her sweatshirt hanging off of her bare shoulder all those years ago.

I kept the thought and stepped into the kitchen for some of the finger food decorating the counter space. I pulled my cell phone from my vest pocket and texted a friend in New York City who knew Pamela well.

"Pamela Berkin is a widow," I wrote.

I received a reply in return: "Tall Jerry and Pamela Berkin—what a match!"

I smiled and stepped over to the groom from all of those years ago and asked him for Pamela's telephone number. He assured me that he would find it for me and asked for my patience while he checked that Pamela was comfortable with my having it.

Several weeks passed before I got the number, and I remember thinking that I was about to turn seventy and wondering whether I really wanted to do this and get rejected or whether I wanted to just go live in a log cabin in a woods somewhere and write words and books. When I first summoned the courage, dialed Pamela's number, and heard her answering machine, I thought about hanging up but left a message.

Several days later, I received a voicemail phone message from a voice that could have only been Pamela Berkin's. Even after all of these years, I haven't forgotten what she said.

"Hi, Jerry. Pamela. So good to hear from you. I'm in the country now but will be back in New York on Tuesday. Give me a jingle after Tuesday, when you have the time. Ciao."

I came home from work on that Friday at around seven, intent on calling Pamela. I looked first at the paper calendar on my writing desk, and then I went downstairs and looked at a clock in the kitchen for the time, and then I searched for any other excuses to stall. While getting a box of Ding Dongs out of the pantry and milk from the refrigerator, I rationalized that she must have been busy, especially since it was a Friday evening, and that it might be awkward for her to talk. I concluded that perhaps I would call the next day.

On Sunday morning I tore the string and wrapper off of a new Jackson Pollack print that I had found on sale at the Vietnamese lady's pictureframing store, which was next to the Chinese takeout place on North Hall Street at McKinney Avenue. I hung it and then put the hammer where it belonged, next to my orange juicer and panini press on a shelf in my pantry, grabbed a halfempty pint of butter pecan from the fridge, and went upstairs to the third floor, stalling for even more time. I unplugged my cell phone from the charger. I went downstairs again to get my thermos of coffee and a spoon for the ice cream. This time I sat in the Carolina chair in the living room, and with my back to the piano, I faced the fireplace, which had no one but me to warm. I stood up, walked into the kitchen, put the pint of butter pecan back into the freezer, and flipped the spoon on the counter. I went again to the chair, sat down, touched the cell phone's buttons, and pushed "call."

My heart began to float like ice cream does in root beer when I heard her voice. I sat up tall. It was a deeper voice than I remembered, but her annunciation was crisp, and her words, succinct and distinctly Pamela. It was a formally friendly, inquiring, happy voice. After all of my fussing over what her first word to me after thirty-five years would be, I had my answer.

"Hello?"

Hearing it gave me a sense of composure—and turned that composure into confidence. I thought of Fifty-Eighth Street and of the iron-elevator ride to 5W and of the tall ceilings. I began to remember who I had been back then.

"What would you like for Christmas, darling?"

"Breakfast at Tiffany's, with you. And you, Jerry? What would you like for Christmas?"

"A walk in Central Park with you."

"That could be arranged."

Pamela and Tall Jerry spent the next two hours speaking of our favorite movies—*Now, Voyager* was hers, and *How to Steal a Million* was mine—and of books we preferred and said not a single word of our time apart or of the years that had passed us by. Pamela spoke of Hemingway's *A Moveable Feast* and of how she would hold the book in her arms as though it were a teddy bear, and I said that I'd just completed Steinbeck's *Cannery Row* and *The Grapes of Wrath* in five and a half days so that I might be inspired to write. "Goddamn it," I said. "Why can't I write like that?"

We spoke of the new snowflakes on her sill on East Fifty-Seventh Street and of the winter season in New York, and she said that she was going to catch a midmorning train in two days to spend Christmas with her nephew's family in New Jersey.

We hung up with smiles in our voices, and the joy of reminiscing with her warmed my heart like hot chocolate would've warmed my body. I remembered a sweetness that hadn't been familiar to me for nearly a quarter of a century. I went to the garage on the ground floor, got in my car, and drove to the Northpark Mall without turning the car radio on to search out a Tiffany store.

The next morning Federal Express delivered to Pamela's doorman two small, white Irish bone-china hearts on a sterling chain. Artfully embossed on each heart were the words "Please Return to Tiffany & Co., New York." The personal note in the iconic light-blue Tiffany box read, "In case we get lost in Central Park." It was signed "Jerry."

That afternoon there was a voice mail on my cell phone from Pamela.

"It's darling, Jerry. How precious. Thank you. And I promise we'll get lost in the park—I do know it quite well."

"I couldn't resist," I said when we spoke again.

"I'm wearing it as we speak, and a Merry Christmas to you too, Jerry. I'm off to New Jersey tomorrow, but we'll talk soon."

"Oh, we will. Travel safe."

In my more than sixty-eight years of life, I had never had a better Christmas present than hearing the sound of Pamela's voice.

For the next several months, I woke up at five o'clock, showered, shaved, drove into work, and wrote for two and a half hours before starting my job at eight. At six, I would write for another hour, and I would get home by seven fifteen each evening. Then I would dial Pamela, and we would talk about books and movies and the snow on the trees and Paris and Luchow's in New York and its Christmas tree with long, ornamented branches that would hang over your table and the sauerbraten and the pine needles that would drop onto the table linens.

We talked about Pamela's seeing how there was so much snow in the city that people would all hold hands on the streets to keep from falling down, and others would ski to work on cross-country skis. We talked about my daughter and the books I wanted to write and whether she remembered our first kiss.

"I was dialing my Princess phone, calling for a pizza. Oh my. Jerry, what do you remember about me?"

"You had great underwear."

"Well, proper knickers are most important. I've always maintained that."

"Did you love Paris?"

"My heart never left Paris. Have you been there?"

"I've been all through Canada and Mexico, not Paris."

"I lived with some girls there. One of my roommates married that wonderful actor Scott Glenn. They all warned me that boys in Paris would teach me dirty words in French and not tell me what they really meant."

"That must've been good for some laughs," I said.

"Once I spent a weekend on the southern coast of France, and when I returned, I went to an important appointment with the *Vogue* editor in Paris. She wanted to jot something down for me and didn't have a pen. I handed her mine. She tried to click it several times without any success. I naturally assumed that sand from the beach had gotten in it and said, 'Excusez-moi, le stylo est dégoûtant.'

"I thought I said, 'Pardon me, the pen is dirty.' But thanks to some Parisian boy's French lesson, I actually said, 'Pardon me, the pen is shitty.'"

"Did she laugh?"

"She was so polite. She smiled, and in broken English, she said, 'Your French is very good, Pamela.' My friend later told me what I had said."

I smiled into the phone, thinking of the Eiffel Tower and '66 Chateau Lafite Rothschild.

"*Now, Voyager* is on Turner this Saturday. Care to watch it with me…you there…me here?" Pamela said.

"Sure. Do you do movie popcorn?"

"I always do popcorn and Chardonnay for Turner Classic Movies. You?"

"Either sliced cantaloupe or a box of Ding Dongs and a carton of milk. Depends on my mood at the time."

"And your mood is?"

"Won't know until Saturday. It'll depend on whether my writing for the week ends with a period or with a question mark."

"Thinking of me should cheer you up."

"Thinking of you will definitely cheer me up."

"Okay now, be honest. What do you remember about me, Jerry?"

"Hmm."

"I want to see if you really remember me."

"The day I left, you were standing naked on the step stool, adjusting a new shower curtain."

"Oh dear, I had forgotten about that."

"I told you that I'm a writer, and I remember a great deal—especially about you."

"I still have that step stool."

I smiled into the phone at the memory of the morning we shared.

"Send me things to read."

"I will. Greg has read a lot of it. He gave me some good ideas."

"I used to see Greg in Manhattan. We bumped into each other all the time on Madison and on Fifty-Eighth. He's such a lovely man."

"He didn't know a term I used in one chapter, 'butcher paper.' Do you know what that is?"

"Butcher paper? Of course. It's the paper that the man at the meat market wraps your steak or meat in."

"I was sure that since he's from Staten Island, he would have heard it. He hadn't, but I left it in. I knew it."

"Is it difficult, Jerry—writing words?"

"Writing more is easy – writing less is hard. Editors like less."

"Send me something. I have a bad cold that just won't leave me alone, and I want to cuddle up with something warm to read."

The next morning I arranged for the Second Avenue Deli to express deliver four quarts of hot matzo ball soup to Pamela's door on East Fifty-Seventh. The doorman delivered two novellas that would become a part of my first novel to her the day after that.

I would write something and send it and write something and send it. Pamela was becoming my muse—my inspiration. Her comments were frank, thoughtful, and encouraging. If a passage made her warm all over or made her laugh out loud, she would tell me immediately. If one made her cry, she wouldn't call me for two days. She said that I reminded her of F. Scott Fitzgerald and that he was her favorite author overall, although her favorite book was still *A Moveable Feast*, by Ernest Hemingway.

On Valentine's Day I sent her a vase of three dozen long-stemmed white roses. On Easter I sent a full smoked salmon and the fixings from Second Avenue Deli, whose employees, seeing the caller ID, would answer the phone by saying, "Is this Dallas for Pamela?" On her birthday, I sent another vase of three dozen long-stemmed white roses. She loves white roses so.

I don't remember how many movies we watched at the same time or how many long phone conversations we had or how many chapters I wrote and sent to her, but one day Pamela, knowing that it was hard for me to get away from work, hinted that she'd be coming to Dallas. I think it was just after I sent her the chapter in which Mr. Pitts gives young Jerry his kerosene lantern, several wicks, a bottle of kerosene oil, and kitchen matches for an early Christmas present, knowing that he's going to die and won't need them.

"Are you all right with a visit?" Pamela asked.

"Absolutely," I said. "I'll have to see when I can get away."

"I was thinking of coming there. Would you be good with that?"

"I think you'd like Dallas."

When she had her ticket in her hand, Pamela called and gave me her flight information.

"We land at eleven fifteen, but you might give me a half hour or so for customs."

"Pamela, this is Dallas, not Paris. Customs?"

"Oh dear. I forgot. I've traveled all over the world but not so much around the States. Are you near Houston by chance? I was there for a shoot."

"Have you ever flown on a Concord?"

"Oh yes. Did you know that you could leave Paris on a Concord and arrive in New York before the time you'd left Paris?"

"Actually, there is a customs thing here specifically for anyone coming from New Jersey or New York into Texas."

"You're teasing me; I know a tease when I hear one. So how do I sneak into Texas?"

"It's all about your accent."

"Excuse me?"

"You have to talk like a Texan to get in."

"And just how does one who knows Manhattan and Paris talk like a Texan, pray tell?"

"Simple. Just superglue your upper lip to your teeth and gums and talk only using your bottom lip."

"You're not going to make this easy, are you?"

"A chaw of snuff under your lower lip helps. Why, they'll see that bump in your lower lip, and hell—they'll give you a dang armed escort and drive you into Texas in a red pickup."

"Will I see snakes? I don't do well with snakes."

"No snakes. Scorpions and tarantulas maybe but no snakes. At least I haven't seen any in the city."

"Oh dear."

I was sitting by the baggage claim when I heard the announcement that Pamela's plane had landed. I stood, straightened my tie, and watched the hallway from the gates. It had been thirty-three years since we'd seen each other. I recognized her blond curls in the sea of people approaching and started waving like my dad would have. When she walked toward me, Pamela was just as beautiful as she had been on the day I'd first laid eyes on her, in 1966. I swept my arm around her waist and lifted her just enough as I leaned in and kissed her as though I were returning from the war and she had waited for me all of that time. She took it well.

I held her hand like a schoolboy would have, and we retrieved her luggage, found my car in the maze they call DFW, and drove home. I explained to her that this visit was special and that with the exception of a visit to the Kennedy Museum, which I had been to before, we'd do only things that I had never done in Dallas even after living there for more than forty years.

That way, we could experience them together.

I kissed her at the garage door and again on the second floor and, I do believe, on the third floor as well. I remember that my king-sized bed was made up but that half of it was covered with papers. I used it as my filing cabinet, since my writing table was just next to the bed against the back wall. I left the papers there so as to not appear presumptuous, but Pamela quickly picked them up, set them on my desk chair, and tidied the bed.

"I love the colors of your walls and all of the art. You're going to love my apartment in the city. I would hang the pieces I've seen here."

"There's a nice Vietnamese lady with a framing shop up on the corner. She calls me when she gets print shipments in. I try to get things I like. I get Chagall, Matisse, and Miro prints that are signed in the stone. I save big on them—on prints and giclée reproductions—and I frame them well so that they look like originals."

"That's a beautiful grand piano. Do you play?"

"I can play 'Country Gardens.' I bought it before I bought a refrigerator, thinking I would take lessons, but when my sister died, I quit my lessons and started writing."

I enjoyed Pamela's down-to-earth manner. We shared a common zest for living every moment, for experiencing life as eager pupils, and for wondering what life was all about. We both agreed that life ain't about the road—it's about the ride. We agreed on matters of money and material things too. We'd been rich, and we'd been broke, but we'd never been poor. We would keep the books and the art; we wouldn't need much else.

"Well, it'd be nice to have some wine," Pamela said.

"Ding Dongs," I said. "I have milk and boxes of Ding Dongs."

In Dallas we went to the School Book Depository and the Kennedy Museum. Pamela was in awe through most of it and in tears through the rest. It wasn't the first time I had seen the museum, but it was gripping that time as well, to say the least.

While we were downtown, I wanted to show off the original Neiman Marcus, so we went there for lunch. The gentleman who served us was Stanley Marcus's houseman and driver. Stanley had long since died and the company gave him a job for life in that small elegant dining room, at Stanley's request. He was gracious, and he served our brunch on silver with such panache. We followed that lunch with a stroll through the store. When we were in the basement jewelry department, several women came up to us to ask Pamela for her autograph.

"I'm not her," Pamela said.

"You aren't?" one of them asked. "Why, you look so much like—"

"Who?" I asked.

"Carol Channing," the ladies said.

"I get that all the time," Pamela said.

As we found the elevator, Pamela told me that she had had drinks one time with Carol Channing at a party and that neither of them had thought they looked alike.

"How did you meet Carol Channing?" I asked.

"One of my dear friends in my modeling days was David Merrick. We weren't lovers; we were dinner buddies. I would walk to the theater late in the show and watch her come down the stairs in the *Hello, Dolly!* finale. That's how we met, and we had a drink while we were waiting for David. He was the producer of *Hello, Dolly!*"

Not to be outdone, I said, "When I was eleven, I sat on the singer Kay Starr's lap while she sang

'Wheel of Fortune' one time when she came to our house in Delphi Falls."

"Oh my. You were a naughty incorrigible even at eleven?"

I kissed Pamela before the elevator door opened. I liked the way her eyes rolled back in her head.

We went that week to the Dallas Zoo. Pamela adored the sculpture of the tall giraffe at its entrance, but in the three hours we were in the zoo, we hardly saw one animal come out of a den, down from a branch, or out from behind a rock. The overhead train was diverted until further notice because the year before, a wild gorilla had gotten loose, climbed the fence, and boarded the train with a leap—and without a proper ticket.

The icing on the cake of the Dallas visit was our tour of the Southfork Ranch, which was made popular in the television series *Dallas*. We walked into its entrance, which seemed like a small metal building. It had the typical souvenirs for sale. In the back there was a doorway, and on the passageway's floor were six or eight concrete tiles with handprints and footprints of the show's stars. Behind the building there was a tractor attached to a line of passenger carts—perhaps ten or fifteen of them. We walked out back, and three people from Ireland, Pamela, and I waited for the driver and the tour. In time a man came out and climbed into the tractor's seat way in the front. He turned around in his seat with a handheld microphone in his hand and looked back at us with a smile.

Pamela leaned over to me and whispered, "This is going to be a long, long tour. I can tell by looking at Sinatra up there in the driver's seat with his microphone."

The tour consisted of him pointing out every single thing that hadn't been in the television show—and doing so painfully slowly. Inside, the guide had us sit at the round kitchen table and said, "Two years ago a real Dallas fan from the West came and bought Southfork and had it completely redecorated."

"So was anything on the television show even shot here?" one tourist asked.

"The pool, the outside breakfast table, and the driveway and the trees near it were."

The night before Pamela was to leave and fly back to New York, we went to the Pyramid Room for dinner. I was disappointed that it had been redesigned and that it no longer matched my memories of it. It lacked the elegance that it had once had, with its forty foot tall suede covered walls and the wine cellar on shelves that followed a tall chrome ladder at least twenty feet up the wall. Back in the day, you would see Milton Berle with his family at a corner table, Stanley Marcus alone at another looking at a Christmas catalog, and the Pointer Sisters having dinner before their naps and their performance at the Venetian Room.

We got home and were in the library when Pamela knelt next to my chair and nestled her head on my shoulder.

"I don't want to lose you this time, Jerry."

"I'm not going anywhere," I said. "I'll be here. We do great phone."

"I'm certain I'm in love with you," Pamela said. "How do you feel about me?"

"I can't even remember what love is, Pamela. It's been twenty-five years for me."

"What will we do?"

"Let's keep doing what we've been doing. It feels good. Let me run it all by my daughter. We'll be fine."

The next morning Pamela turned and watched my eyes as she walked down the hall at DFW to board her plane. We both felt good about the visit. We both felt good about us.

Three days later I called Pamela.

"Hello?"

"I had a nice talk with my daughter."

"And?"

"She's delighted. She sounded so genuinely happy. She told me to just have fun and to see how it goes."

"I'm going to love that girl."

"Know what else she said?"

"What?"

"She said that she remembers you from the picture with RFK and that she's had your picture on her wall all her life."

"Now I'm going to cry."

"She said she's going to make a copy of it and put it on the visor of her car."

Pamela and I spoke daily, visited each other, and visited friends and relatives off and on for more than a year. Her city apartment was impeccably decorated with custom chairs and fine art on walls of red lacquer that were just like those in my library on the third floor in Dallas. Prints of Pamela donned one wall in her New York apartment, and one that I wasn't particularly fond of because of the look on her face was hung off to the side. I told her I didn't like it and asked her why it was there, and she told me that of the thousands of pictures that had been taken of her, it was her favorite. It was her favorite because she knew what she'd been thinking when the photo had been snapped: "I can't believe they pay me all this money to do this."

It was the night I was in the city with Pamela at a corner table in Canaletto Italian Restaurant on Sixty-First. It was about nine o'clock when Pamela's new cell phone announced that she had a text message. She looked at me with a startle, as she had never received a text message before.

It read "XOXO" and was signed with my daughter's name. Pamela's eyes grew wide, and she beamed.

"How sweet!" she said.

Another text sounded on her cell phone.

"What on earth?" Pamela said, picking up the phone.

The text read, "Pamela, if my godfather asks you to marry him tonight, will you say yes?"

Pamela read the message. Then she adjusted her glasses and read it again as I took her hand and put a sterling-silver heart-shaped ring from Tiffany on her finger. She reacted as though it were a fifty-karat diamond.

"Well?" I said.

"Well, what?"

"Well, will you?"

"Of course I will. Forever and ever…I just can't speak right now."

Pamela held her left hand over her heart with her right hand. A happy tear made its way down her cheek.

We didn't set a date, but we knew we wanted each other for the rest of our lives and went through months of listening to opinions from our friends. I was the one who eventually made the decision.

Pamela came to Dallas.

My daughter, my son-in-law, my godson, and his wife were to be the wedding party. The ladies spent the day at a chic Dallas spa while we men enjoyed manly barbecue and Western-style boots in Fort Worth. Our rehearsal party consisted of taking a Cadillac SUV limo to Medieval Times, where wenches threw chicken legs onto our trays, and armor-clad knights jousted. At that show a knight with a long, flowing red silk scarf raced his black stallion up toward us and threw a rose in the air. It landed squarely on Pamela's hand just as my son-in-law leaned over and said, "This is the best rehearsal dinner I've ever been to."

We were married the next afternoon in the Roosevelt suite, which had a private elevator and two balconies, at the charming Rosewood Mansion on Turtle Creek. A Catholic and a Lutheran who were very much in love got hitched by a Baptist minister on his own anniversary. My daughter was the maid of honor, and her husband, a grooms-man. My godson was my best man, and his wife, the official photographer.

We said "I do" and simply turned around. The men kissed the bride, and we sat at the table in the suite for an evening of food, festivities, warm cheer, and cake.

From the moment that Pamela and I came back into each other's lives during that Christmas telephone call, life has been magical for us both. She is my muse—my first thought when I wake up. It's as if we were separated in time but never in thought. We love each other passionately, enjoy the same art and the same books, and still hold hands like we're going steady and kiss on street corners as if we're in Paris. We believe in guardian angels. Pamela, an extraordinary cook, makes salads that would challenge the Waldorf. Whether Pamela is preparing a dinner of French roasted chicken or I'm orchestrating an Italian carbonara or Philadelphia's epic 'Revolutionary' hot-cabbage salad, we listen to jazz or vintage big-band music, embracing spontaneously and dancing between the dings of the timer. Then we sit to dine, unfolding our linen napkins and our memories. We look into each other's eyes, and I still see the twenty-three-year-old girl I met in Bellerose, and she still sees that young man who followed her over to the stout Louis XIV–style bureau on Fifty-Eighth Street, held her cheeks in his hands, and boldly kissed her. We hold each other the entire night, folded together like delicate pastries. And we wake to more smiles, more memories, and still more kissing.

The wedding anniversary at this writing, seven books after we first reconnected, I bought my lover and my bride four dozen long-stemmed white roses. Several weeks later, she was sad to see them wilt. I got her four dozen more.

As for my never wilting love for my Pamela—well, there's plenty more where that comes from too.

Photo Credit: Bo Joplin

Pamela and Tall Jerry and their tingly-all-over love

RICHARD LEAVES THE CHOIR BREATHLESS

I can't think about Christmas without remembering my first Christmas adventure with my brother Dick in 1947, the year before we moved to Cazenovia. I was six years old. We were living in Cortland, and I was in the first grade at Saint Mary's Catholic school. We were a family of ten – Jim, me—Jerry, Paul, Dick, Fred, Mike, Dorothy, Mary, Mom and Dad. Being the next to the youngest –I learned early on to take things into my own hands if I wanted to get something done, and not wait to be asked but to make decisions that helped others if I could, and to just assume that at least half the family won't notice anything I do, and the other half won't care.

It was a still–dark early school morning. I wasn't dressed yet and crawling under my sister's bed. I had to find my marbles. It took ten marbles to play in a "keepsies" game in back of the school—one for every finger and thumb. So far I had one for each finger and my Steely shooter. I had to find my marbles. My sister Dorothy had babysat me the night before, and while I'd been playing with them on her bed, my string on the bag had come loose, and they'd spilled out of my marble bag while I'd been asleep. They'd fallen off of the bed with each toss and turn and had rolled all over her floor. So far I'd found a hairbrush with dog hair on it and a candy-bar wrapper.

It would have been a lot scarier in the dark under the bed if I hadn't been able to hear all of the talking going on in the house. It was the day the sisters—the nuns—were going to pick the pupils who would be in the Saint Mary's Christmas pageant. I could hear Mother downstairs telling Mike not to be disappointed if they didn't pick him for something, as he'd played "Michael McNamara, the leader of the band" in the Saint Patrick's Day pageant. I could hear her telling Fred to be certain to stay with me in the school yard so that my knickers wouldn't get spoiled, which surprised me. I didn't like wearing knickers, because I had to wear knee socks with them, and Mother had to pin my knee socks to my knickers to hold them up. I liked wearing my short pants better. I figured that maybe she'd forget about my knickers if I kept as quiet as I could under there. I could hear her telling Paul to remember to keep his collar buttoned and to sing his best.

"Where is my Richard?"

Mother started to come up the stairs.

"I need to see my Richard."

"Here I am, Mom," he said, stepping out of the bathroom and wiping the wet tooth powder from his mouth with his sleeve.

Mother ran a comb through Richard's hair. "Now, Son, you are my straight A pupil—with the exception of deportment."

I didn't even know what the word "deportment" meant at the time, but I figured it couldn't be good.

"Try to be a gentleman, young man; I just know it's in you somewhere. Do your very best to behave, dear."

"Yes, Mother," he said.

Nobody else got a talking-to like that. Richard was really smart, but he was always getting into trouble for something, so I guess he had to be warned to behave more than the others. When Mother asked him what he was going to do for the pageant tryouts, he said, "I'm going to sing my solo, Mom."

Well, if he'd said that to any of his brothers or sisters, they would've wondered what he was up to, but when Mother heard it, she just imagined him getting on stage in front of a million people who were cheering and clapping and yelling "Bravo! Bravo!"

I finally found enough marbles for my thumbs and all of my fingers, but I just stayed under the bed, listening.

"Dorothy? Find Jerry, please, and let's get him dressed for school."

I didn't know it, but Dorothy had been sitting on her bed putting on her makeup the whole time I'd been under there. All of a sudden, her hands grabbed my feet, which must have been sticking out, and started tickling them. That got me out, and she pulled me out too, which helped.

Dorothy started dressing me and pinning up my knee socks to my knickers so that they wouldn't fall down my skinny legs.

She lifted my school cap off of her bed and handed it.

"Do I have to wear my hat?" I said.

She looked at me, smiled, took it from my hand, and said, "Absolutely not, my dahling!"

And with a twist of the hand with the pretty nail polish on it, she flipped the hat way up over her head, and it hit the wall behind her and bounced back down onto her bed. She leaned back and put it under her pillow, out of sight.

Then she gave me a big kiss on my cheek, got up, and held my hand as we went downstairs, where I knew Mother would tell me how handsome I looked and give me a hug and some breakfast.

I hid my marble bag in my pocket so that it didn't draw too much attention to me and get taken away from me until school ended. Fred was supposed to walk me to school and watch me until school started. That was good because Fred liked to watch me play marbles, mostly because the older girls liked to watch the really young kids play, so he pretended he did too. I wasn't as good at "keepsies marbles" as some of the other boys were, but I got some more marbles in my bag almost every time I played.

Dick and Paul had their books wrapped in belts slung over their shoulders and ran ahead, but Fred and I walked down Helen Avenue, along the path through the field at the corner, and then to Saint Mary's school. When we got there, we walked around back to the playground, and sure enough, some boys were shooting marbles. I put my Steely shooter in my pocket so that no one could see my advantage and held my marble bag by the new string so that the boys could see that I had enough to play.

"Want to play?" one of them asked me, looking up from the ground.

He scooched over.

"Yes."

I got my shooter out of my pocket and counted out marbles with my fingers and thumbs. "I'm in," I said.

I lost some marbles quickly to the boy with a cat's-eye shooter. He was good. I kept moving around the circle that had been drawn in the dirt, trying to get a better position, and I won a marble back.

All of a sudden, Fred picked me up off the ground and put me on top of the big brick post between the fences. Then with his hands, he brushed dust off of my knickers and straightened my knee socks, which were then stretched out from kneeling.

"You're getting your clothes dirty, and I don't want to get into trouble."

He left me up there on the brick post while he turned, knelt down, and got the marbles he thought were mine.

Now, I worried about my brother Fred a lot, because he was really smart about some things, but he didn't always think about what he was doing. I wasn't certain whether it was because of the girls or because he just forgot to pay attention, but while he was putting my marbles in my marble bag, the school bell rang, and he just turned around and walked into the school, leaving me on top of the brick fence post all alone.

I would have started to cry if I hadn't seen Sister Mary Francis looking out the window at me and moving back and forth, all flustered.

The sisters, or nuns, as some people called them, had black-cloth capes and hood on their heads, like the Virgin Mary, and white starched cloths all around their faces and foreheads. It always seemed that they were looking through holes in sheets that had been ironed and starched real good and pulled tight around their faces, and all of the sisters looked the same walking away. Sometimes you could tell them by their walk. Their belts were giant rosary-bead chains that wrapped around them and hung almost to the floor.

I could tell that it was Sister Mary Francis, because I knew the kind of glasses she wore. She kept leaning over, first in one direction and then in another, to see whether someone was outside with me. Then both of her hands went way up in the air and to her face like she was slapping both cheeks.

"Oh my goodness—that poor child!"

She disappeared, and I didn't see her again until she came out through the back door and lifted me down off of the brick fence post.

"I'm coming, Jerome, you poor dear. What on earth possesses young people at times? Heaven only knows."

She mumbled something else under her breath, but I couldn't make it out. I didn't think it was a good time to bring up the fact that my brother Fred had my marble bag. I could only hope he wouldn't lose it.

When we were all in our schoolroom at our desks, we stood and said the Pledge of Allegiance and then prayed. "Art Father, who art in heaven," we said. I never understood why everyone called baby Jesus's father Art, which was the name of the man who worked in Aunt Agnes's grocery store. I thought baby Jesus's father was Joseph.

Then we prayed some more. "Hail Mary, full of grease," we said.

I never did get them straight until my first communion.

Sister Mary Francis set a book down in the middle of her desk, dinged her bell, and told the class that we were to line up and go to the auditorium that morning because they were picking children for the Christmas pageant.

"I want complete silence," she said. "Everyone do just as you are asked to do."

First she lined us up and walked us to the lavatory. She waited outside the boys' lavatory door and inspected us to make sure that we'd buttoned our pants. "Did you wash your hands?" she asked. "Don't dawdle, children. Did you wash your hands?"

We boys shrugged and gave her convincing "uh-huhs" even though some of us couldn't reach the faucets.

When we walked into the auditorium, a lot of older students were already there. Girls were standing in aisles, brushing their hair, and boys were opening gum wrappers and making a lot of noise. We just got in our seats and watched and listened, wondering where they'd all learned so many things to say and whether they'd ever run out of things to talk about.

Kids made a long line on the side of the stage, the girls trying to straighten their clothes and the boys rubbing the tops of their shoes on the backs of their pant legs to buff them up. A sister came out from behind the closed curtain, walked over to the piano, turned the lamp on it on, and sat down.

One at a time, kids walked out to the middle of the stage and did things for the sisters to hear or watch. Some handed the sister sheets of music to play on the piano while they sang. One girl in pigtails walked to the middle of the stage, held a pigtail under her chin with one hand, raised the back of her other hand, leaned it gently against her forehead, closed her eyes, and loudly said, "Romeo, Romeo, wherefore art thou, Romeo?"

A voice in the back of the auditorium responded. "He went home!"

The girl startled, stomped a foot on the stage, broke into sobs, and ran off stage right.

The auditorium roared. Instantly the curtain on the stage-left side ruffled as the mother superior stepped out onto the stage like a hurricane, leaving the tall velvet curtain, which was the reddish color of a nosebleed, rippling and swaying back and forth behind her. She stopped center stage and stood there as straight and as still as a cold marble statue with both of her hands on her hips and her elbows sticking out sharply like weapons. She stared into the audience, looking for the boy who had yelled out a response. Like an owl looking for its prey, she rolled her head slowly to the left and slowly all the way to the right. The audience considered itself warned. She walked back offstage and behind the curtain.

Some of the kids came out and tap-danced to music, wearing special shoes with metal noisemakers on them. Some came out and played songs on the piano. One girl played the accordion, and one boy played the flute—at least until someone threw paper balls at him—and a boy with his pants unbuttoned played the violin. A lot of the kids sang songs.

When it was Dick's turn, he walked out on stage adjusting the bow tie that he had thought to put on at the last minute. At the middle of the stage, he turned toward the audience, walked to the very front of the stage, and took off his glasses. He rubbed them around and around on the front of his shirt while his eyes slowly looked the audience over. He gazed up at the ceiling as if he could see it without his glasses, which he couldn't, and then he slowly put them back on and began clearing his throat as though he were a big opera star. He was going to sing a solo, so everyone quieted down while he cleared his throat.

"Ahem…ahem. Ahem."

"Richard!" the mother superior said in a loud, crackling, blood-curdling whisper from behind the curtain, warning him to stop stalling. "Sing your song!"

He turned and corrected her. "It's not a song—it's a solo!"

Then he began.

"She came riding down the mountain doing ninety miles an hourrr when the chainnn on her bicycle broke.

Well, they found her in the grass,

'cause she landed on her ass,

and her tit was—"

"Not one more word, young man!" the mother superior said.

Dick didn't get to finish the line. He didn't get to sing as much as one more note or finish his rather catchy song. With an audience screaming and roaring in laughter and uttering gasps of every kind, the mother superior—who had heard the "a-s-s" word—bolted out from behind the curtain and flew across the stage. Her big black nun's cape was flowing behind her like a massive condor, and with one deadly stretch of her arm, she reached for Richard. With a thumb and a finger especially trained for just this sort of anarchy, she grabbed and pinched Dick's left earlobe so tightly that it actually seemed from our seats that she had lifted him up off of the ground. He was at least up on his toes, and in a series of swift motions, she quickly led him offstage by his ear.

"Ow…ow…ow…ow. Ow…ow…ow…ow."

With each step he took, Dick uttered another "ow" amid the audience's roars and laughter. Every time she tugged on his earlobe, his toes would go on point on the stage floor, and he'd skip like a ballerina. With her right hand, the mother superior clasped her giant rosary beads, which were balled up like a snake, though they usually swung in the air. She did that to keep from tripping on them, but it seemed that she was going to use them to tie Dick up, and then, when they were behind the curtain—well, who knew what would happen then?

"You are in so much trouble, young man. You are incorrigible, and we are calling your mother immediately."

Then I thought I heard her growl.

"Did he say really say 'a-s-s' and 't-i-t'?" some of the kids said.

They spelled the words out so as to not get into trouble themselves. Others said he was going to go to reform school. One boy wished he had sung that song to get out of the pageant.

I asked Sister Mary Francis what "porrigible" was, and she snapped at me and told me to sit down.

When the noise subsided and Dick was in the principal's office, we all had our turns. The sister told me that I would be reciting something from "'Twas the Night before Christmas" and holding a bowl with jelly in it, which was good with me, because I liked the story. The sister said she would write down instructions for what I was to say in the pageant and what I was to bring, and she would send them home with my brother Fred. That didn't make a lot of sense to me, 'cause he'd just forgotten me in the school yard and would probably forget my marbles somewhere—especially if there were girls around.

I was worried about Dick, though, and I didn't want him to go to reform school. When we walked back toward our classroom, we walked by the mother superior's office, and I could see Dick standing in the corner, which was what they had kids do when they'd been bad. Back in class, Sister Mary Francis told us that school would be let out right after we drank our orange juice, because we all had to go home and help our families prepare for Thanksgiving.

I knew I had to make up a fib to keep Dick from going to reform school, so I walked up to Sister Mary Francis's desk.

"Sister, my mother wanted Richard to walk me to the shoeshine parlor after school to get my shoes polished for Sunday Mass, and she really wants him to walk me because his are scuffed too."

I turned my bottom lip down. I thought that using the name Richard instead of Dick was a nice touch, as Mother would have called him Richard—even though she probably would've decked him for what he'd done. The sister stared at me, first in one eye and then in the other, the way grownups do when they're trying to determine whether you're telling the truth. Then she turned sideways in her chair as if she was about to get up, leaned toward me, and glanced back into my eyes again just for confirmation. I was stoic. She stood up, took me by the hand, and walked me to the mother superior's office, where she closed the door behind her and spoke. Dick peered around at me with one eye while he pressed his head against the corner and grinned just quickly enough for me to see it. His forehead had a patch of red on it from being pressed against the wall.

Dick had actually learned how to take a nap while leaning on the wall like that, as he'd had so much practice. The longer the nap, the darker the red patch on his forehead would be.

Sister Mary Francis came out from the mother superior's office, took me by one hand, took Dick, and put my hand in his.

"We will deal with you another time, young man."

She looked at him sternly, leaning down almost to his face with a warning eye, which he could hardly see through the glare of the sun reflecting off of her glasses. She pressed a pointed finger on his nose as if it were an elevator button.

"But now you must walk your brother directly, and I mean *directly*, young man—do you hear me?—to the shoeshine parlor on Main Street and get your shoes polished for church, as your mother told you to do."

"Huh?" my brother said, looking a bit confused.

"Move!" she said, snarling. "And mind you, hold his hand all the way and when crossing streets too, young man. Now march!"

Dick kept looking over his shoulder (which was something he did a lot when he was in school) as he walked me out of the building and down the front steps. We crossed over to the other side of the street and walked in the direction of the shoe-shine parlor. He looked bewildered. I told him I'd made up a fib to get him out of the mother superior's office so that he wouldn't have to go to reform school, and we didn't have to go to the shoeshine parlor. He smiled, paused, and checked his pockets to see whether he had any money for a soda.

He didn't.

We turned down a side street and walked toward home. He didn't say a whole lot on the way home, but he knew forever, from that very day on, that his little brother would do everything he could to keep him out of reform school. I think I was begin-ning to understand what the word "deportment" meant and how Dick got in trouble with it.

I also knew how much I loved my older brother Dick, even though the sisters thought he was "porrigible" and even though he got deported a lot, or so I thought at the time.

Postwar Shortages and Shortfalls

I saw two cars through the gate. My sister Mary was in the green '49 Oldsmobile with her husband, Don, who was driving, and my other sister, Dorothy, was in the Chevrolet with my brother Mike. This close to Christmas, all of the siblings who were either in college or married always headed home to spend the better part of a week and to wait for Santa with us. They were coming to the falls for our first Christmas in Cazenovia. I was eight. Mom watched them roll through the snow from the window and shouted in glee. Everyone in the house—Paul, Dick, Fred, Aunt Kate, Mom, and I—went to the door in our pajamas to greet them. It was a few days before Christmas, and the spirit of the holiday was officially alive in our household.

There were colorful ribbon hard candies in some bowls and every kind of nut and nutcrackers in others. My sisters played Glenn Miller records. They also played Christmas songs and sang carols, and we all sang around the piano. Dorothy and Mary took turns reading stories to us at night while we had hot chocolate, popcorn, and roasted marshmallows if we were lucky.

Mom greeted everyone with her arms open wide.

"Hang your coats; come to the table. Your father's at work, but the bacon's ready, and we'll make pancakes."

The boys sat around the table listening to Mary, Dorothy, Mom, and Aunt Kate, who were in the kitchen all talking at once, pouring orange juice, and sipping their teas and coffees.

"Even with the war over, Mom," Mary said, "there are so many things that are still impossible to find. With all of the war shortages, nothing's back to normal yet when it comes to shopping."

Mom agreed and reminisced about the sacrifices that everyone had made for the war effort and about how some sacrifices, like rationing sugar and gas, had been more noticeable than others.

Mom held her coffee cup with both of her hands.

"Thank God it's over, though—especially for all of the boys and girls who were out there in harm's way. Mary, I thank God every day that your Don came home safe."

"I remember that every household got ration stamps or coupon stickers for its car's windshield. Remember that, Mom?"

Mom snickered.

"Some sacrifices were even less noticeable—like rubber, which meant elastic. Girls, do you remember that certain garments, like pajamas and underwear, didn't have elastic in them during the war?"

"All because of the rubber shortage?" Mary asked.

"They had buttons or drawstrings instead," Mom said. "It was a battle just trying to keep them up."

"Speaking of certain garments, Mom, Dorothy and I have presents for you and Aunt Kate. We want you to open them right away," Mary said.

Don and Mike were busy carrying in firewood, and the rest of us were watching, listening, and waiting to eat.

"You girls didn't have to," Mom said.

My sisters always went together to buy things for Mom and Aunt Kate—things for them to wear through Christmas. This year they had bought pretty flannel nightgowns and had decorated them by hand, sewing jingle bells and candy canes all over them. Along with the flannel nightgowns, they each got a pair of shiny red satin panties. Mom opened her box, held up the nightgown, and saw that it reached her knees. She held up the red satin panties, which looked like the flag of a fire truck, and we boys all hid our eyes until Mom asked, "What's this?"

We each looked up with one eye open, not wanting to miss a thing.

"That's a ribbon tie," Dorothy said. "It's for your panties."

"They were on sale," Mary said.

"After you pull them up, tie that ribbon just like you'd tie a pajama string, and they'll stay up," Dorothy said.

We boys rolled our eyes and hoped that someone would interrupt this lacy diatribe and announce that it was time to eat. Mom, our sisters, and Aunt Kate carried on and talked about panties like we weren't even in the room.

Then they went to Mom's room to put them on.

Dorothy and Mary played the record "White Christmas."

In the middle of breakfast, just as Mom was saying that it was going to be a lovely white Christmas, she paused and looked up at the ceiling.

"Oh dear," she said. "I forgot to go to the bank for your father. It closes at twelve because of the holiday, and he'll be home early today from his trip to Carthage."

"Mary and I are going to Cazenovia to do some last-minute Christmas shopping," Dorothy said. "Can't we go for you?"

"No," Mom said. "The bank's in Tully."

With that, she stood up.

"I'll take the younger boys and run over there. Paul, Dick, Jim and Jerry, get shoes and coats on."

We each grabbed as much bacon as we could.

Now, there was one thing you could do in the country that you could almost never do in the city, and that was put a coat on over your pajamas and go outside. There was hardly any chance that anyone would see you. If someone did, he wouldn't look for long, because he'd have to keep his eyes on the road for deer.

Mom was in her brand-new flannel nightgown with candy canes and jingle bells on it and, we assumed, wearing her fire-engine-red panties. She put her overcoat on and walked out of the house in her slippers, carefully following our tracks to the car.

"There will be absolutely no one at the bank this close to Christmas," Mom said on the way to the car. "Climb in, boys."

It was my observation that a girl could put a coat on over a flannel nightgown, and no one would ever know she was in her pajamas. A boy in his pajamas, on the other hand, was easy to spot, so I hoped nobody saw us.

The Tully bank was on a corner. The bank was a big place—or at least it seemed big to us kids—with tall ceilings and Roman pillars. It had a marble floor that shone, as it was waxed daily. You could slip on it if you weren't careful. The bank was one large foyer with desks arranged on the carpet, and there were cages at the counter, where people counted money or made deposits.

As I recall, we kids usually hated having to go to the bank, because we had to be quiet and well behaved there.

But this day was different. We needed to be patient because the next day was Christmas Eve. We resolved to just go in like good boys with Mom so that she could do some banking for Dad. He probably needed some last-minute Christmas money for a turkey or something.

Mom parked the car. When we got out, she had us line up like geese and follow her up the snowy front stairs, which a man was shoveling, and in through the two big doors. Inside, we walked over to a mahogany table in the center. The table had glass on top of it so that people couldn't scratch the wood or spill ink on it. It was almost as if we were in a church—it was that somber and big. There was a beautiful Christmas tree decorated with colored lights that reflected off of the ornaments and shiny silver icicles. There were more people in the bank than Mom had expected there to be. Some ladies walking by us saw our pajamas and smiled. Some said, "Merry Christmas," and some looked at us as if we were the Kettles, the hillbilly family of movie lore. It was embarrassing for a boy, but at least my brothers were in their pajamas too.

That's when it happened.

All of a sudden, Mom lifted her head up, looked straight forward, and, with her voice trembling, said, "Oh dear."

"What is it, Mom?" Dick said.

But he'd barely gotten the words out of his mouth when she said, with more authority, "Oh, Lord." Then Mom, who was still looking straight forward, said, "Children, circle close around your mother this minute. Hurry, please!"

We boys knew that that really couldn't be good. It never was when Mom called herself "your mother."

All of us did exactly what any curious young boys in our situation would have done: we took two steps back to look about and see what had happened.

"Closer," she said again, her voice trembling.

Then the suspense was killing us—that is, until a little boy walking by looked down, quickly assessed the situation, looked up, and, in a most articulate, matter-of-fact voice, announced what had happened so that the entire bank could hear him.

"Hey, look! Your mommy's panties fell down! Your mommy's panties fell down!"

Mom wanted to die. We felt her pain, and although we wished we were dead, we moved closer to her to keep people from seeing. She must have forgotten to tie the ribbon drawstring well—or at all, for that matter—and what had been done had apparently been undone too.

I knew that tying pajama strings could be tricky. One time my jammies fell down to my knees in the kitchen while I was reaching up into a cabinet for some peanut butter, and I was "full moon over Miami," as my dad liked to say, until I got them pulled back up.

My brothers and I looked around the bank; nobody was looking at us. By that time Mom's panties had hit the marble floor and were billowing like one of the parachutes in the Saturday morning newsreels about D-day. Then they came to rest and flattened out on the marble at her feet.

"Want me to get them, Mom?" Dick asked.

With that, the woman did something that amazed us, and we talked about it every Christmas following that one. As she stepped out of the panties with the dignity and grace of a mother of eight who had figure skated before thousands when she'd been in her early teens, she took control of the situation and told my brother Paul to stand behind me. He did it immediately, as that took him farther away from her panties, which then lay flat under her feet on the shiny waxed floor of the bank. Without another word, Mom raised her ankle sideways in a move reminiscent of an Olympic skating turn, closed one eye, and beaded at an empty desk right by the front door, which was about ten feet away. With one fast swipe of her foot, the fire-engine-red satin Christmas panties slid like a fire engine on ice all of the way across the bank floor until they landed under the empty desk by the door and were completely out of sight. Mom had actually kicked her panties ten feet across the marble floor of a crowded bank without anyone seeing her do it. We truly were amazed. We almost applauded. Of course, we were humiliated—that goes without saying.

"Everyone to the car," Mom said.

We didn't need to hear that twice or to receive encouragement of any kind to get out of that bank. As she walked by the desk, Mom leaned down, reached under it, picked the panties up as though she had dropped a Christmas scarf, and stuffed them into her coat pocket. We were out of the bank in a flash. We boys left with our eyes bugging out as big as quarters and our mouths hanging open.

If it had happened in Fabius or Delphi, where everybody knew us, we would have left town that afternoon.

At home, Mom told Dad, Dorothy, Mary, and Aunt Kate what had happened and what she had been forced to do to keep from being totally mortified. Dad smiled.

"That was good thinking, Mommy. You still have those magic ankles. I can do my banking on Monday," he said. "There's never a holdup at the bank when you need one, is there, Mommy?" he added.

Dorothy started giggling and kept giggling so hard that she had to run to the bathroom. Aunt Kate had tears streaming down her cheeks from the laughter. Mary was laughing so hard that she couldn't breathe, and her face was as red as a beet.

The Tully bank never looked the same to any of us ever again.

A Cazenovia Christmas Past

We lived in dairy-farm country in upstate central New York after the war ended, and our house was less than a hundred yards away from a loud seventy-foot-tall waterfall in Cazenovia, the Delphi Falls. The property came with eighty-four acres of untillable cliffs of rock and shale and fossils, with pine and maple woods, and with a second falls upstream on Limestone Creek. The land had no commercial value to the dairy, wheat, or cabbage farmers in the area, and that's why my father was able to buy it from the county for $3,000 toward the end of the Great Depression, when no one was looking. The county used the large wooden pavilion for the county park's public picnics and Saturday night square dances.

After the war, my dad converted it into a home for the ten of us. Throughout the war, with material shortages for the war effort, no construction was allowed. We moved there from a three-bedroom, one-bath home on Helen Avenue in Cortland. Jimmy was the youngest. Then there was me—Jerry, then Paul, Dick, Fred, Mike, Dorothy, and Mary. By then, four of the eight children in my family – Fred, Mike, Dorothy and Mary were off either in college or married with their own families. Still at home were Mom, Dad, Dick, Paul, Jimmy, the youngest and me—Jerry.

My story begins in March 1954. My thirteenth birthday was coming up, and spring would follow it. We were coming out of a harsh winter—a winter that had brought with it more snow days than usual. On this day the sun was lying to us again, promising a thaw but turning its back on us and letting the cold, brisk winds freeze what little snow had melted. There was a hard, glassy crust on top of that snow, and it cracked like ice when you stepped on it, your feet sinking into the powder below.

Dick, Paul, Jimmy, and I came home and stepped off of the school bus to a new midday blanket of powdery white snow covering that morning's lingering melting crust. We rarely spoke when we walked to or from the school bus, and we were walking in a single-file line down the long unplowed driveway to the house when a car that we didn't recognize started driving in our direction just as we caught sight of it. It drove from the house down the crusted, snowy drive. We saw the silhouette of a man in the backseat—a passenger—and based on his stature, we knew that he was our dad. A stranger was driving, and someone who appeared to be a hospital nurse was sitting in the front passenger's seat, wearing a white starched hat and collar and a navy-blue coat. We stopped walking as the car approached us and bent down to look in through the closed windows as best we could in the glare of the afternoon sun. Dad held his hand up in a motionless wave. The car's windows were closed tight, and without hesitation, the car kept moving toward the gate. It didn't slow, it didn't pause, and it didn't stop. We each turned around and watched as the car drove off.

I speculated that it was too windy and cold out for him to open his window. Or maybe he wasn't feeling well—he'd been coughing a lot lately. Maybe they were going to the doctor to get him some penicillin.

We saw Dad turn around in the backseat and give us a gentle, sad wave. His eyes were squinting from the tears I saw glistening in the sunlight through the rear window. Dad was weeping, and I didn't know why—or even where he was going. We stood and watched him out of respect, just in case he was still watching us, until the car turned down Cardner Road. It picked up speed and drove out of sight. I remember wanting to cry. Our dad had looked so sad, staring back at us. He had never left us in such a manner before, and we had no idea why he was being taken away—or why he hadn't stopped to talk. We ran as fast as we could into the house to find Mom standing in the book den, staring out the front window with tears in her eyes.

"Where's Dad going?" Dick asked.

"Why wouldn't he talk to us?" Paul asked.

"Why was he crying?" I asked.

I'd never felt quite as alone as I did at that moment. Without taking her eyes off of the long driveway, Mom told us to go get out of our school clothes and to meet her at the table. She'd made hot chocolate for us to drink while we talked. After we changed, Mom summoned us into the kitchen to get our cups and to take them to the table. Seeing us together made her smile a little. I think that that was because we were home, and she wasn't alone anymore. Mom hadn't been separated from Dad since the day they'd met and fallen in love, in 1919.

She sat at the end of the table.

"Boys, I have something to tell you. I need you to be strong and to be my men of the house. We'll get through this together."

The phone started ringing. We let it ring.

"Your father and I chose not to tell you about what I'm going to share with you now until we were certain. We didn't want to worry you unnecessarily. Your father has tuberculosis, and it's a bad disease. When he passed you on the driveway, the hospital nurses were driving him to the TB sanatorium, where he'll stay until he gets better."

"Is that why he was coughing so much, Mom?" Dick asked.

"Yes, dear. Tuberculosis attacks the lungs, and it affects breathing."

I started to tear up. "Is that why he wouldn't talk to us or say good-bye?" I asked.

"Oh no, Son, and I don't want any of you to think that. Please don't think that for a minute. It's just that they don't know a lot about tuberculosis. They think it may be highly contagious in the early stages, like polio, but they're not sure. Once the people from the sanatorium came today and told your father that they'd confirmed that he had TB, he couldn't and wouldn't risk exposing you to it. That's why he could only wave to you. He loves you so much—he would never leave without saying good-bye to his children if he didn't have to. Your dad even asked the driver to wait until he saw the school bus come so that he could at least wave good-bye."

Our minds could get around that a little better, but the air was still tense. Dick, Paul, Jimmy, and I couldn't conceive not being with our dad ever again.

"When can we go see him?" Dick asked.

Mom looked down at her hands to gather her thoughts.

"I'm so sorry, boys, but you can't—not until he's better. Not until they've confirmed that he isn't contagious and know that it's safe for you to see him. Just pray for your father every day. Pray that he will come back to us healthy and strong."

"How long will Dad be gone?" I asked.

Mom looked at each of us. "It could be a year. It could be—"

Knowing the statistics and that TB was the number-one killer in America, Mom started weeping; she was a strong woman, but her face dropped into her hands. Dick jumped up and ran into her and Dad's bedroom and came back with the handkerchief I had given her for Christmas years earlier.

"Thank you, dear," Mom said.

She looked down at the tabletop and kept dabbing her eyes as if to avoid eye contact, which she knew would start her tears all over. We stood, quietly pushed our chairs in, and walked toward Mom. We each put a hand on her shoulder as we walked by and went to our own rooms. I lay down on my bed and stared at the ceiling. I kept thinking of Dad looking around in the rear window of the car, weeping as he waved. I turned over and buried my face in the pillow so that no one would hear me cry.

The next day was Friday. When the school bus came, we weren't out at the gate. The bus driver, Ralph Scullens, honked a few times and then drove off. None of us, not even Mom, got out of bed until later in the morning. Mom, who would normally make us walk to school if we missed the bus, didn't say a word about our missing school that day. She felt that it was a time for us to all be together, and she wanted us close to her in case any of us had questions. The house was quiet all day. Dick sat on the floor, looking in the encyclopaedia so that he could learn about tuberculosis. Paul stayed in his room, listening to his radio, and Jimmy rolled an edition of *Grit* newspaper for delivery on Saturday. When it was time for supper, we went into the kitchen and fed ourselves. For most of the afternoon and even just past dark, Mom was on the phone talking to our brothers and sisters about Dad's going to the sanatorium and about TB. Dick made a salad for Mom, warmed up two meatballs he'd found in the refrigerator, and put them on a plate in case she was hungry. None of us kids said a word that day. I walked around in a trance and looked out windows and teared up when I walked by the picture of Dad on the piano or the one of him on the wall in the hallway.

After dark we went to bed again. I knelt down by my bed and prayed so that my dad would get better, not be in pain, and be home for my birthday, or at least for Christmas. I prayed so that he would come home.

The next morning Mom was smiling when she woke us up. She had made breakfast, and she asked us to come eat, as it was already on the table. It was as if she were a new person. She told us that God would answer our prayers. It was Saturday, but she got us out of bed and told us that it was time for us to be strong, that our dad had been through worse than this in his life, and that we should have confidence in him. With the Lord's help and our prayers, she said, he would get through this.

"What was worse than this, Mom?" I asked.

Mom looked around at each of us and told us something that we'd never heard before. She asked us to not bring it up unless our dad did first.

"When your dad was just a boy like you, Jerry, his father fell from a barn roof in Minnesota and died. It was a difficult time," she said. "Your father was the youngest of seven, and he was so hurt by losing his father that he could never bring himself to talk about it or think about it."

"Is Dad going to die, Mom?" I asked.

"Your dad would want you to do the best you can in everything you do and to go on with your lives just as he taught you to. If you do that for him, it will give him the strength he'll need to get well again."

We promised that we would.

"Can I write him a letter?" I asked.

"It would be better to tell me things for him. I'm allowed to visit him, and I can relay what you want him to know and any other news to him. That way, he and I can talk for longer during my visits, and I can keep his spirits up. I can keep his mind busy with the things that we want to tell him. It's important to make sure that he stays positive and wants to get better and come back home."

We all understood that.

"I'm going to camp out," I said.

"In the snow?" Dick asked.

I got up from the table, went to my room to get dressed, and grabbed my knapsack and the kerosene lantern that Charlie Pitts had given me the year he'd died.

I felt like a grown-up all of a sudden, not like a kid anymore. I couldn't explain it. I just somehow didn't feel the same as I had before. I grabbed my knapsack and bedroll and headed out to the barn. Our two horses were standing close to each other, sharing body warmth, and soaking in the morning sun but not moving or eating the broken bales of hay lying on the ground before them. Horses can sleep standing up, so I wasn't sure whether they were asleep. I slid the stable-barn door open and went in, stuffed my knapsack with as much hay as I could, and got Jack's saddle down off the rack. I brought it to the open doorway and set it on the floor. I went back to get the saddle blanket, paused, and walked back to the door to look out at my horse. Jack was a tall gray gelding who loved rides, and climbs up our hills didn't bother him. His winter coat was still thick and feathery even though it was March, and he lifted his head and looked at me like he was waiting for me to make up my mind about whether we were going to use a saddle or go bareback. It made no difference to him.

"Bareback," I said out loud.

I put the saddle back on the rack and threw the saddle blanket over the stall door, where it belonged.

I adjusted the straps of my knapsack, hooked the lantern to them, and put it on my back. I stepped out of the barn-stable and slid the door closed. I put Jack's bridle on him and led him away from Major's side—Major was Dick and Paul's horse—because I needed space to jump on his back with the help of a cinder block.

We rode down the long driveway, down Cardner Road, across the small bridge at the creek, and into the snow-covered alfalfa field that Molly, the workhorse, used to call home. The lumber people had taken Molly with them for other work, but they told us that someday soon, they would bring her back.

Jack raised his head high, his nostrils flaring and expelling puffs of morning air. He shook his head as though he were waking himself up. He knew we were going to climb the steep hill that led up to my campsite. He liked to go camping with me. I felt that he knew that on the snow-covered ground, his footing wouldn't be as sure as he would've liked it to be. We got to the back edge of the field. I decided to hold on and to see if I could stay on him while he climbed the hill. Jack's thick coat helped my legs get traction, and the bare, leafless trees let me see well. I squeezed tight with my thighs and legs and held a piece of his mane in my grip. Jack's nostrils snorted steam as his legs sprang forward like claw hammers, pulling us up, and his hind legs pushed up like springs, kicking snow back until we reached our trail at the top, which was more level with our campsite. Clouds of vapor were pouring from his nostrils as though they were steam engines.

We got to the site, and I slid off his back, dropping the reins to the ground. I removed my knapsack and looked about in the snow near where I thought my fire hole was buried for a spot where I could sleep. The hole was covered in snow. I dragged my knapsack around a rectangular patch of ground to move the snow away. Once the hole was clear, I packed the remaining snow to the ground with my feet. I hung my knapsack on a tree branch, started to gather logs, and made the fire bigger than usual so that there would be more heat for both Jack and me. When it was going on its own, I gathered and stacked enough wood to take us through the night.

I mounted Jack again and told him that we were going for a ride. When I was on his back, I realized that for the first time, I'd mounted him with no help of any kind.

We headed back deeper into the woods by the upper waterfalls, which were frozen over with a thick crust of solid ice. A little water was trickling over the falls and dripping down the massive icicles that were melting slowly in the morning sun. I rode through the woods to the back fence of our property line and turned left to go north as far as we could—a ride I had never done on horseback. It was a longer ride than I had planned. When we came out of the woods and into a clearing, we were across from Charlie Pitts's old place. I rode

Jack to the edge of the field that faced the road to Charlie's property, and we stopped. We just stood there. Jack snorted puffs of steam as if he recognized it. I remembered my friend Charlie. I thought about all of the good times that he and I'd had together. How I would walk to his place every week to collect the eggs for my mom. How he would let me play in his barn. How nice he was to us all of the time. I remembered that when he got sick, Dad would come back from work to drive him to a hospital in Rochester every two or three weeks so that he wouldn't be alone during his treatments. I wondered whether Charlie had had tuberculosis.

A tear blurred my vision as I thought of Charlie and wondered what I would do if my dad ever died. I pursed my lips in frustration, wishing that both he and Dad were with me right then and that we could all go ice fishing up at Pleasant Lake.

A breeze kicked up, and Jack turned and followed our tracks back to the camp. I took his bridle off and hung it with the knapsack. I stacked more firewood. I had two blankets, and with the fire, they were all I needed. I unbuckled the knapsack and pulled a quarter of a bale of hay out of it. I'd known I wouldn't want to eat, so I hadn't packed any food for me. Jack leaned his head down, smelled the hay, and then lifted his head up, turning it toward me to thank me. He started munching on it. His back leg sprang up as he relaxed. Horses can lock their knee joints. They'll balance on three legs, keeping one unlocked in case they have to move suddenly in the night. Horses' natural predators are wolves. Their defense is speed.

I didn't need the lantern. I sat on a log by the fire and made some mourning-dove calls to while away the time and warm my hands.

"Whoo-eee, who-who-who. Whoo-eee, who-who-who. Whoo-eee, who-who-who."

I watched a squirrel carry an acorn up the side of a tree and wondered where he had buried them for the winter.

As the darkness hovered, I unrolled my blankets and, lying back, watched the stars over the creek side of the cliff and listened to Jack munching on his hay.

I looked at the silhouette of a single dead leaf hanging from a branch and twisting in the wind, surrounded by a full moon above, and I wondered what my dad was doing.

I wondered whether he was coughing a lot.

I wondered whether he was losing any more weight.

I wondered whether we would ever go fishing again.

I made the decision that I wasn't going to talk about this with anyone at school other than Holbrook, Barber, and Penoyer. I knew my friends. They wouldn't bring it up unless I told them I wanted to talk about it. We knew one another like that—that was why we were such good friends. We were like brothers. Holbrook, my best friend, loved my dad too.

I fell asleep knowing that the rest of the school year and the next fall wouldn't be the same. School would never be the same again for me with my dad gone.

On Monday I was walking down the school hall, pulling my jacket off, when I noticed a girl I'd never seen before. She was walking in my direction, looking like she was lost. She was tall and slender with curly dark-brown hair. She was wearing a plaid pleated skirt and an emerald-green sweater over a white starched blouse. She had a pretty, sparkling smile, and I could see a smile in her eyes as well. I told her my name and asked for hers. She told me that she was Judy and that she was new. She was from Baltimore, Maryland, and would be staying until next November while her parents were traveling or something—I don't quite remember.

She was staying with her uncle, Ted Dwyer, who lived across from the Conways' farm.

I asked her whether she had a locker.

"Not yet," she said.

"Use mine," I said. "I never lock it. I hope that's okay."

"I don't need locks," she said as she placed two books on the top shelf, hung her green sweater on one of the hooks, and closed the door.

"Thanks, Jerry. Nice to meet you," she said. She smiled, turned, and walked away.

When I got home that day, a letter from my brother Fred, who was at Cornell, was lying on my bed. In it he said that he was going to send me new words to look up in the dictionary, learn, and use in sentences. The first word was "pedantic."

I didn't know what it was, so I got the dictionary and looked it up. The second was "copious." The third was "prevaricate." I found it fun, and his letters and words took my mind off of worrying about Dad.

On Saturday I saddled Jack and rode down past Doc Webb's place to the end of the road and up the back hill to the big corner that we called Gooseville Corner. Just across the road was Ted Dwyer's place, where Judy would be living until she had to go back to Baltimore.

I rode onto the snowy front yard, dismounted, and knocked on the door. Judy came to the door. "Want to go for a ride?" I asked.

"Hold on while I put something warm on. Want to come in?"

"Nah, I'll wait out here."

When she came out, I mounted Jack, took my foot out of the left stirrup, and offered her a hand so that she could climb up. Then she was just behind the saddle with her arms around me, holding on. I knew that Judy was older and in the tenth grade and that I was in the ninth, but it didn't matter. I liked her. We were on my horse riding back down the hill to my house for some hot chocolate. We passed the Reynolds' and Cardner places, the Chubbs', the Butlers', and then Doc Webb's. Doc waved and shouted for me to check out his new syrup cabin when I had a chance. I waved back to signal that I would, and we rode on past him.

Mom was at home when we got there. She said hello to Judy, and they talked about Baltimore while I warmed up some milk. I had put Jack, still saddled, in the barn-garage with some hay, so he would be okay for a little while.

We drank hot chocolate, and Judy and Mom talked.

Later I walked Judy out behind the house to see the waterfalls even though they were frozen over. We walked back down to the barn-garage, and I brought Jack out so that I could take Judy home. Before we mounted him, Jack moved his head around and nuzzled Judy as though he liked her and wanted to say hello. Judy put one hand under his chin and with the other stroked his velvety nose and then patted the side of his neck. They became fast friends.

On the way back to the Dwyers', Judy rested her head on my shoulder. I could hear her humming a song that I couldn't make out, but I liked hearing it. We didn't talk the whole ride back. She held me and kept her head on my shoulder.

When we got to her house, I took my foot out of the stirrup, and Judy slid over so that she could reach it.

She held onto the back of the saddle and swung around slowly. I turned to help her, and she paused, looked me in the eyes, and kissed me. She gave me a wonderful, long, warm kiss. Then her head moved back, and she looked in my eyes again and said, "I had fun, Jerry. Thank you for thinking of me." She lowered herself to the ground, rubbed Jack's nose to say good-bye, ran to the house, and waved at me just before she closed the door.

I thought that if it weren't for Dad's being at the TB sanatorium, growing up could be a good thing.

When I got home, my world was shaken again. Mom was packing a small suitcase. She told me that the sanatorium had called while I was out riding and that Dad might need surgery. They wanted to remove a part of one of his lungs. She had to go stay near him for a couple of days while he went through some tests and they talked it over with the doctors.

Mom kept packing and told me to tell my brothers to please be mature and to behave while she was gone. She said that she would be back in a few days and that I should be certain to bring the milk in shortly after it was delivered so that it wouldn't freeze on the porch.

After she drove out of the gate, I walked behind the swings and opened the door of Dad's Oldsmobile, which had been sitting there unused for all of that time. I sat in the driver's seat. I thought of him sitting there. I grabbed the steering wheel as though I were driving. I could smell him in the car. I thought about wanting him to meet Judy.

I went inside and heated up a tuna-fish-and-noodle casserole for Dick, Paul, Jimmy, and me for when they got home.

I told them about Dad and the operation that he might have to have—about how they might have to take some of one of his lungs out.

Dick said he didn't think someone could live without both lungs.

I bolted around in a blind rage, ran toward him in the hall, and pushed him back up against the wall so hard that his head bounced off of it.

"You take that back!" I screamed. "You take that back right now!"

Dick stared at my fists, my clenched jaw, and the tears in my eyes. I just gave him a cold stare. He apologized.

We went to our rooms to calm down.

Judy and I went riding as often as we could. I didn't know what love was, so we didn't talk about that—I just knew that when we were together, we were happy, and when we weren't together, we couldn't wait to be together again.

One time when Mom visited Dad, he told her how to get me a job if I wanted one. I said I did. He said Dick could get one too if he wanted a summer job away from the Lincklean House hotel where he scrubbed pots and pans part time. She told us about their talk at supper. Dick and Paul and I were all for it, so Mom said she would take us to the place on Saturday and introduce us to the owner so that we could see whether it would all work out. She said Dad wanted it to be a surprise, so she would tell us about it when we got there. It would be for the whole summer, from Memorial Day to Labor Day.

On Friday night I went to a school dance with Judy. We danced the slow dances. We even square danced when they played one that sounded easier than most.

I told Judy that I would be looking at a summer job that my dad had arranged. I said that I didn't know anything about it yet, as he wanted it to be a surprise. Judy told me that she was praying that Dad would get better. She was nice like that.

On Saturday Mom drove us to a place called Snook's Pond, near Manlius. It was part of a spring-fed lake that was used as a swimming hole in the summer. It had a long wooden pavilion with men's lockers and changing areas on one side of the pond and another with ladies' lockers on the other side. At the end of the pond was a concrete walkway with chairs on all three sides and a diving board. Just at the entrance to Snook's Pond past the unpaved parking area were two small square huts that had large wood-flap shutters. When raised, those shutters, which were held up by wooden poles, exposed the serving counters on the front three sides of the small shacks. One of the shacks was where people paid to get in and to rent lockers. The other shack was a snack bar. You could get hot dogs, popcorn, and soda pop—all you wanted in that one shack.

Mom introduced us to Mr. Snook, who walked us around the property and gave us a tour. He told us that the jobs consisted of running the snack bar and going around the grounds to pick up empty bottles and papers and rake up cigarette butts three times a day. He said that we could work there, but we'd have to work seven days a week from Memorial Day, when they opened for the summer, to Labor Day, when they closed for the winter.

"Do you want to think about it, boys? It's quite a commitment," he said.

"What does it pay?" Dick asked.

"Nothing," Mr. Snook said. "Didn't your dad tell you?"

"No," Dick said.

"You'll run the snack bar as though it were your own," Mr. Snook said. "You'll keep any profits you make. How does that sound?"

"We'll take it," Dick said.

On the way home, Dick asked Mom to ask Dad to make a list of what he thought we should buy to stock it, where we could buy it, and how to pay for it.

The summer flew by. We took turns cooking hot dogs in the steamer, selling things, and swimming whenever we wanted. I got to drive the orange Allis-Chalmers tractor and wagon from our snack stand to the storage garage down the driveway to get cases of soda pop. The day after Labor Day, summer was over. I walked all around the place to do a final pickup, knowing that I would probably never see it again and that I would miss it. I thanked the place for helping us pass the time so that we didn't just mope around, worrying about our dad and missing him.

When we pulled up to the house, I ran out of the car, saddled Jack, and trotted down to the Reynolds' hill and up to Judy's. As soon as she opened the door, I took her by the hand and led her out to Jack without saying a word. I started to mount him, and she said, "Hold on a second, mister."

She took my face in her hands and gave me a kiss.

"I missed you this summer. Did you have fun?"

We rode for a couple of hours around the Conways' and Dwyers' farms. We never stopped talking. I told her about all of the crazy people we'd seen at Snook's Pond and about how to make twenty hot dogs at once so that they were always hot and fresh. She told me about the books she'd read and said that she was getting sad because she'd have to leave soon. I didn't want to talk about that, so we just rode. She held me close.

School started the next day.

Mom had arranged for me to go visit Fred at Cornell. It was his junior year. I had grown almost seven inches since spring. Fred had invited me to come up for a weekend and to stay at his fraternity house. I packed a bag. Mom drove me to Ithaca and dropped me off. The next week was Thanksgiving, so he told Mom that he would drive me home for that.

The weekend went by quickly.

As soon as we got home and walked in the door, Mom asked us to join everyone at the table, as she had some news.

"Your father and I thought it best not to worry you, so we didn't tell you that he had his surgery last Friday. I'm happy to tell you that your father is doing fine, and with prayers and hope, he could be home by Christmas if he heals well and if there are no complications."

I remember looking at Mom to see whether she was comfortable with what she was telling us or whether her eyes were nervous and maybe hiding some bad news. She was smiling.

"The doctors make him cough several times a day to keep his lungs clear. It's painful for him, but he knows that he has to do it, so he does his best."

"Does he still have two lungs?" Dick asked.

"Yes, they only had to take the top portion of one of his lungs—so he still has two lungs."

We were so happy, and we couldn't wait to see our dad again after almost a year. There was a holiday dance at the school that night. Mom drove me and stopped to pick up Judy. She and I danced all night. I thought that it might be the last time we got to dance, since she might have to move back to Baltimore any day.

We were busy with our family during Thanksgiving, and not long after that, I started to get letters from Judy. She had moved back. Her parents had come during the school break, gotten her with no warning, and given her no time to say good-bye. She wrote me a letter, and I held it all night. We wrote back and forth for months. I missed her— but I missed my dad too.

It was the morning of Christmas Eve, but the house didn't feel Christmasy at all. There was plenty of snow on the ground. We usually hoped for snow at Christmastime, and it was still snowing, but the house seemed cold and still and quiet.

I got out of bed and went to the kitchen in my pajama bottoms and T-shirt. Dick was already there.

"I'm making your favorite, Jerry," Mom said.

I knew it was poached eggs. Mom knew I loved poached eggs. I would put one on a slice of buttered toast and eat it like an open-faced sandwich.

Mom asked if we could help fold the clothes right after breakfast so that we'd be ready for Christmas and said that we'd let everyone else sleep in. She told us that Don and Mary were coming from Harrisburg that day with our nephews, Tommy and Timmy. Our sister Dorothy and her husband, Norman, were coming in from Washington with their daughter, Karen. Mike would arrive soon.

Noticeably, Mom made no mention of Dad. We were afraid to bring it up so early. We didn't want to make her cry. We knew that if Dad couldn't come, it would be out first Christmas ever without him. We all felt the same way: there wouldn't be a Christmas without Dad.

We moped around the kitchen, eating, talking, and folding clothes as Mom piled them on the counter. It was almost two o'clock, and I was still barefoot and in my pajama bottoms and T-shirt. Dick was looking at the pile of presents lying by the piano. Paul had walked into Delphi Falls to see his girlfriend, Joanne Davenport. Mike had driven in and was sitting on the piano bench playing "Volga Boatman," most of which he had memorized.

I went to my room and fell asleep.

The next thing I knew, Mom was pulling on my toe. "Jerry, get up. Get up—your dad is coming home! Your father's coming home!"

I sat up and rubbed my eyes. It was dark outside. Mom had a smile on her face. I wasn't sure whether I was dreaming or really awake.

"Mike Shea just called and told me that the man who's driving him home stopped at the store and went in to buy your dad a newspaper. Mike went out to the car and said hello to him. He said your dad looks good, and he thought it would be nice to call us and let us know that they're on their way—the man and your dad!"

I stood up. I could hear Dorothy and Norm laughing and talking with Dick and Mike in the living room. I brushed by Mom and went to the bathroom.

When I came out, I looked from the hall through my bedroom window. My sister Mary and Don were driving in with their lights on and with a Christmas tree tied to the roof of the car. I'd thought that we weren't going to have a tree that year. I started walking down the hall to get dressed when the telephone in Dad and Mom's room rang. I rushed in and picked it up.

"Hello?"

"Hello, is Jerry there?"

"This is Jerry."

"Jerry, this is Dr. Webb. Merry Christmas, young fella. I thought you would like to know that your dad just drove past my place on his way home. I thought you would like to know, what with it being Christmas and all."

"How did you know he was coming?" I asked.

"We old fogies have our own SOS system, don't ya know," he said, laughing. "We invented it. Have a bully good, merry Christmas, son!"

I dropped the phone receiver to the floor, ran out through the dining room and past Dorothy and Norm to the front door, and opened it.

Mom shouted for me to put something on, but I was already out the door.

I jumped off of the front step and started quickly walking, still barefoot, through the snow toward the gate. I kept my eyes on the top of the road up by farmer Parker's hill, looking for the headlights of the car that Dad was in. I knew that the car that Dad was in would be coming over that hill at any minute.

As I scurried past her, Mary opened the window of her car and shouted, "Jerry, you will catch your death. Go put something on."

I kept walking as fast as I could, keeping my eye on the top of the hill.

Finally, almost at the gate, I saw the light beams and a car coming slowly over the hill, inching around the curve. The road was unplowed and slick, so they were taking their time. I stepped out onto Cardner Road. The car turned into the driveway and paused for a moment. The back window opened halfway, and a hand reached out of it to shake mine.

It was my dad.

It was my dad!

I grabbed his hand and squeezed it as I walked alongside the car.

"Jerry?" he asked.

"Yes."

I tried to hold back a weep. I'd grown almost seven inches since he'd last seen me, and I hadn't been sure he would even recognize me. It had frightened me to think that my dad might not remember me.

"Remember fishing at Little York Lake, Dad? I rowed us out in the boat at Sandy Pond. Remember? Do you remember when you beat my airplane to Watertown, Dad? Remember teaching me how to make desserts? Do you remember me, Dad?"

The car came to a stop at the house, and the family was on the porch waving and cheering, and Dad squeezed my hand and said, "You caught crappies that we cooked at the Imperial House. Remember, Son?"

"Room number six," I said.

"Room number six," he said.

He remembered me.

After the car stopped Dad got out carefully. He stood slowly, as he was still tender and healing from his lung operation. When he stood up straight, he looked at me and at how tall I was. He ran his hand back and forth over my brush cut.

"You sure have grown, Jerry, me boy. You sure have grown."

I stared into his eyes.

"I'm still the same, Dad—just like you're still the same."

He shook my hand and put his arm around my shoulder, and we walked into the house with sounds of cheering, laughing, and crying all around us. We were all happy again.

"Go take a warm shower so that you don't get frostbite," Mom said.

"No! I'm not leaving Dad!" I said.

"Well, at least go put some pants and shoes on."

I did, and I got a sweater and came out and sat on the chair next to the couch where Dad was resting, smiling again, and watching everyone talk at once.

Don, Norm, and Mike were putting up the Christmas tree, and Mary, Dorothy, and Mom were bringing out boxes of decorations and lights.

Dad asked Dorothy for some writing paper and a pen or pencil. He wanted to write a friend in the TB sanatorium to wish him a merry Christmas.

I remembered when I lay on that same couch on the day I was poisoned from drinking water from the creek. I remembered Dad sitting where I was sitting then—sitting tall and watching over me all night long, his silhouette crested by the moon's glow.

I sat up taller in the chair.

When I woke up, it was still dark outside. The house was quiet, and all of the lights were out except for the ones on the tree. The Christmas tree was a spectacular glow of lights and colors and shiny, reflective decorations. Presents were stacked underneath it, and Dad was still on the couch with a blanket over him. He was holding the pen in his limp hand, and the paper was resting on his lap. But he was asleep.

I took the pen and paper off of him and put them on the arm of my chair.

His eyes opened, and he smiled. "Can I have some water, Son?"

I got him a glass of water from the kitchen.

"Want a fire, Dad? I know how to build a good one."

"That would be nice, Son."

I moved his papers to the seat of my chair and built a big fire with the largest logs, remembering the time I left ears of harvest cow corn right there by the fireplace for Santa.

I stacked enough wood to take us through most of the night. I wasn't certain of the time, but I knew that everyone would be getting up soon to celebrate Christmas.

I walked back to the chair. Dad was asleep again. I picked up the paper and pen and sat down.

I didn't read Dad's entire letter, but I did read one paragraph:

I'm sleeping on the sofa for my first night home just so that I can be in the thick of things for Christmas in the morning. My boy Jerry is roughing it on a less comfortable chair right beside me while he and I catch up. He doesn't seem to mind. Watching him snooze makes me recall the many nights he used to sleep on a bedroll over the falls here at Delphi when he camped out. The horses would come around grazing or just snooping late into the night. Jerry didn't mind horses, woodchucks, squirrels, rabbits, foxes, deer, some bears, or the load of wild birds that roamed the upper falls sometimes.

I remember looking up at the glowing tree and over at the burning fireplace.

As I watched my dad sleep, a tear rolled down my cheek. "There is a Santa Claus," I said. "He came tonight."